THE ROYAL RING

Printed in the United States of America: First Printing, 2022.
ISBN 978-1-7378376-6-4 (eBook)
ISBN 978-1-7378376-7-1 (paperback)

http://www.hannahwillow217.wordpress.com

Copy/Line Editor: Wes Imrisek
Developmental Editor: Angela Grimes
Cover Art: Getcovers.com
Formatting: R. L. Davennor

CHAPTER 1

"You'll never catch me!" Jamie yelled as she ran down the path, leaves crunching under her feet. She heard the pounding soles of the girl behind her as she darted around the turn in the path, heading for the treehouse. Her lungs burned and she gulped in more air.

As the structure came into view, she upped her speed, leaping onto the ladder, and climbing into the house in the sky. Once at the top, she heaved for breath. A stitch stabbed in her side, and she toppled over onto her back. She gazed through the treetops to the cerulean blue sky dappled with white clouds. A light breeze tickled her face.

A laugh preceded her friend, who fell down next to her. "That was not fair!" Her proper voice, so at odds with the twelve year old body it came from, said, "I've never even been here before. Of course you were going to get here first." Star smiled and Jamie felt lighter.

Jamie snickered, lifting her knees to plant her feet flat on the floorboards. "Isn't it wonderful?" She rolled her head to the left and gazed at Star. Her black hair pooled around her head, and her blue eyes sparkled. Jamie didn't know if she'd ever seen anyone so pretty.

Star, short for Anastasia, came from Ixica, a small country in Europe, and her family was visiting to experience an average American Thanksgiving. They happened to come to her small town in Wisconsin and while out playing, Jamie ran into Star and they'd hit it off right away. A week into Star's vacation, and the two of them were thick as thieves, and just as mischievous.

Smiling sadly, Jamie stretched out. "I can't believe you're leaving tomorrow. Will I ever see you again?"

Star rolled over to her side, bending her knees up and curling her arm under her wavy black hair. "It feels like I just got here, and also like I've known you forever, Jamie. You're not like the girls back home. You treat me like . . . I don't know, just like me." Though they spoke the same language, Star sounded regal when she spoke. Her accent thrilled Jamie.

Every now and again Star would talk like this, but never

said much more about back home. She wanted to learn about America, not talk about Ixica. Jamie breathed in the scent of pine trees and fall in the Midwest, the cooling air, and a bonfire somewhere in the distance. Suddenly, Jamie sat up. "Do you smell that fire? I bet that's coming from the campsite. S'mores!"

Star gazed at her quizzically as she pushed herself up to sit. "S'mores? What are those?"

Not believing what she'd heard, Jamie gaped at her friend, jaw slack. "You really don't know what they are? Graham crackers with chocolate and a roasted marshmallow all smooshed together into a sandwich? It's only the best thing ever!"

With narrow eyes, Star leaned back on her hands. "I don't know if that sounds good or like the grossest things I've ever heard of. Are you sure this is worth tasting?"

Jamie jumped to her feet before she reached down to take Star's hands. She tugged until they were both standing. "Come on, trust me on this one. Have I ever steered you wrong?"

Star continued to stare at her with narrowed eyes. She tilted her head. Before she could speak, Jamie put up her hands. "Wait, you can't hold cheese in a can against me, we specifically went into that store looking for something gross. I don't even eat that stuff."

With a huff, Star relented. "Fine, I'll give you that. And that was the only really disgusting thing we've tried. Okay,

I'll try *one* of these s'more thingies and if it's awful, I'll just know it's all your fault."

"Deal!" Jamie said with a smirk, "And if you *don't* like them, I'll know you have no sense of taste…and more for me!" She made her way back down the ladder.

The two walked and skipped back down the trail to the campsite her family had rented for the last night Star's family would be in town. It was a weirdly warm weekend for the end of November in Wisconsin, but they had an RV so even if it got chilly, they'd all be sleeping indoors.

When they got back, both families were sitting around the large campfire. Star's two younger brothers, Malcolm and Adrian, sat by their parents while they discussed some adult thing with Jamie's parents. Malcolm, a few years younger than them, shot them a dirty look. With his black curls, he looked a lot like Star. "Why did you two go without me? I thought you were bringing me!" He crossed his arms over his chest, and his lower lip jutted out.

She slumped. Jamie wasn't sure what to say, but Star didn't have that issue with her brother. "Malcolm, it's our last day and we were gone for maybe ten minutes. After this weird concoction we'll go back out and take you with us."

He perked right up at that.

"All right," Mom said. "Time for s'mores. Jamie, you can teach everyone your best strategy."

Jamie leapt up and, taking a step forward, she took 'center

4

stage.' "Okay everyone, we each need a stick. It needs to be about three feet, or um...a meter long. This is for roasting your marshmallow without burning your hand."

Adrian, small for his nine years, shot Jamie an apprehensive look, his bright blue eyes getting moist with tears, then he turned to his parents. "I'm not so sure I want to do this."

Jamie bit back a laugh, and gave him a reassuring smile. "Don't worry, you'll be fine, and it's *really* worth it."

After that, they all went out and found sticks. Jaime modeled how she roasted the marshmallow, and soon everyone had white pillows of sugar rotating over the flames. Her dad prepared the graham crackers and chocolate so that once the marshmallows were ready, everyone could eat.

Star gingerly took her first bite and her eyes grew to the size of saucers. "Oh...wow! That's amazing." She lifted her hand to wipe the sugary goo from her lip into her mouth. "Just lovely. Can I make another?"

Once everyone had eaten their fill, Jamie and Star took Malcolm to the treehouse. While he climbed up, Star held Jamie back. She gazed at where she held Jamie's hands, shuffling her feet, and not saying anything. After a minute, Jamie got worried. "Everything okay, Star?"

Her head shot up, and Star's shiny blue eyes, bright like a gem, got wide. "Yeah, I mean yes, everything is perfect. I was just wondering." She paused to stare into Jamie's eyes.

"You two coming up?" Malcolm yelled from the treehouse.

"In a minute," Star yelled back, not breaking eye contact, then she released a puff of air she'd been holding. Speaking fast, as if that would help, she said, "I was hoping to give you a kiss, if that'd be okay with you."

For a few seconds, Jamie forgot to breathe. She got lost in the blue depths of her friend's eyes, and nodded. She'd never kissed anyone before, but she liked the idea of kissing Star. When Star smiled, her face lit up as bright as her nickname. Star angled in and gently brought her lips to Jamie's. As soft as it was, Jamie felt tingles straight to her toes.

Star leaned back, a smile blossomed across her face. "If we were older, I'd want to marry you, Jamie Woods."

Jamie's mouth fell open. "But why? You're so amazing."

Pulling a ring from a chain around her neck, Star handed it to Jamie. Jamie looked at the pretty trinket. It would be too big for her finger, but the fines and leaves were pretty, and there was a 'I' in the center. Star explained, "This is a promise ring, my signet. It binds us together, and wearing it, it will remind you that you're amazing, too, Jamie. Don't forget it…okay? And one day I'm going to come back for you."

CHAPTER 2

14 YEARS LATER

The horse pounded down the trail, and Anastasia pulled out her bow and an arrow. Up ahead, a field came into view, where she'd heard a wild boar had been spotted killing a farmer's chickens and goats. Lifting up slightly from her saddle, she squeezed in with her knees to stabilize herself and nocked the arrow, ready to aim. She loved shooting from horseback.

Trailed by security, her group broke out of the part of the train in the trees into the field. The beast stood almost a meter in height in the center of the field, with black, rough-looking fur, and two small tusks. She drew the arrow back, took a calming breath as she aimed, and loosed the arrow. In a matter of seconds, the wild boar went down and cheers went up from the two security men following her on their horses. Being the Royal Princess, heir to the throne of Ixica, there were very few places she could go without a security escort.

Clean-up wasn't her job, so she slowed her horse to let gamesmen pass by her. They steered their mounts out to gather the boar and talk to the farmer as she turned back towards the woods. It wouldn't take long on the path to return to royal lands, and she could head back without much of an entourage. She found her brother Malcolm on his horse with the remaining security staff as they headed back to the castle.

Somehow he found a way to lounge on his horse, with his shoulder-length black hair tousled from the ride. He smirked at her. "Nice shot, sis. Do you wanna go talk to the family yourself, be the hero of the day? I'm sure speaking with the next queen would make their day…probably their year."

She stopped her horse, Stardust, and shook her head. "I'm no hero, and I'll be late for my appointment, as you well know, brother. Are you going to stay and watch, or come with me?"

"Oh, you know I'm with you. Appointment," he scoffed. "I don't know how you spend all your time volunteering at that school. All those kids." He shivered. "Don't they drive you batty?"

Anastasia shook her head and kicked her horse in the direction of home. Tall, old trees shadowed the wide trail, and she and Malcolm could ride abreast of each other. Birds sang deep in the woods, a backdrop to their conversation.

"The kids are a joy, and their sounds, while loud and piercing, are happy sounds. You should come with me sometime; it's not as bad as you think it is. You'd have fun…you know, like the kind of fun you used to have with Adrien and Finley."

He shivered at the memory before glaring. "Don't remind me of those days. At least when Finley visits now, there are fewer pranks. He more or less leaves me alone."

"Well, he did grow up, Malcolm, just like you."

The two rode in silence for a few minutes, enjoying the peaceful pathway through the countryside. Once they got away from the commotion of the field, the familiar path through their lands relaxed Anastasia. The bird songs and the scent of the apples growing in the orchard reminded her of younger years. She turned to Malcolm. "Have you talked to Pa about your job and Jordan?"

"Have you told Pa about your interests, then?"

Body stiff, she shook her head. "I don't know what you're talking about."

"Oh! And I say this as respectfully as I can, stuff that, sister mine." He laughed. "You know exactly what I'm talking about, but if you're unwilling to admit it, even to me, I won't push it. But no, I'll tell him once I'm world famous. It doesn't matter; you're the one who'll take over the throne, not me. I'm free to follow my joy, or whatever those silly Americans say."

Shaking her head, Anastasia smiled at him. "I'm glad you're doing what you love, Malcolm, but you really should let Pa know, and Mum. I'm sure they'd be fine with it. You've always been their favorite."

Malcolm's head fell back as he laughed loud enough to quiet the birds. "Me? The favorite? That's Adrian, and you know it. With his pranks and the way he's always playing, you'd think our parents would tire of him, but oh, no, always the favorite, that scamp."

"Don't be jealous, Malcolm. They love you, too. So, if you won't come to the school with me, how about archery practice later this afternoon?"

With a huff, Malcolm gave his opinion of that. "Why must you choose all these horrible activities? Such violence! I do love spending time with you, Star, but small kids and arrows are not the way to my heart. Why couldn't you have taken up baking? We could spend the morning making cakes."

"That does sound lovely. I do admit, but my last attempt in the kitchen didn't turn out so great. It's a good thing we have cooks and a master baker. Fine, you go run off with Casimir and learn what you can. Has he approved any of your designs?"

Eyes alight with excitement, Malcolm turned as far as he could in his saddle to look at her. "He has. I was told I could run with a tux-inspired evening-wear design I came up with. Casimir even said it was worth exploring. He says he may add one or more of the designs into his next show." He practically vibrated with his announcement.

Anastasia gaped at her brother, then narrowed her eyes at him. "Why has it taken you this long to tell me? That's amazing news! When will you design something for me to wear?"

They broke out from the tree line and headed for the stables. The warm sun peeked out from behind the clouds. "I'll get you something once Casimir approves of my designs and tells me my work is worthy of royalty. If you were anyone else, I'd have made you something already, but you're the Crown Princess, soon to be Queen. If I put something on you and it's a failure…well, so am I."

As they got to the stables, one of the stable hands came out, wearing black slacks and a crisp white polo. His neat blond hair and brown eyes twinkled as he gazed at Malcolm. Anastasia leapt down. "Hi, Jordan. Please give Stardust an extra carrot. She performed admirably today."

Safe on royal grounds, security rode into the stables to get their mounts put away.

Jordan yanked his gaze from her brother and bowed his head. "Yes, Your Highness, of course."

She handed her reins to the stablehand as Malcolm quickly checked to make sure they were the only three in the yard.

Malcolm reached out, brushing his finger under the other man's chin, and bent down to kiss him. "I'll see you later tonight."

Jordan grinned before he led the horses away.

Anastasia and Malcolm turned towards the house. Anastasia grabbed Malcolm's hand. "You're going to get him in trouble for being so open. He could get fired."

"Poppycock! He's too good at his job, and we're very discreet…normally."

"I worry you don't know the meaning of that word. Again, if you'd just tell Pa, then none of this would be a worry, would it?"

"Star, stop meddling—"

Adrian ran up to them from the main house, breathing hard, eyes wild. "Star! Malcolm! Come quick! It's Mum. She said she needs to talk to us. Something's happened to Pa!"

CHAPTER 3

Jamie leaned closer to the mirror and carefully applied the last of her eyeliner. She'd pinned back her brown curls with sparkling bobby pins she'd ordered for tonight's fancy night out. The eyeshadow, which went from gold to bronze in an ombre effect she'd read about in a magazine, brought out the green in her eyes and dress.

She'd bought a jade green and black dress, interwoven over her chest and torso in a hatched design. The dress itself was an A-line cut that dropped down to a flared out skirt. The skirt glimmered with jade green and clear crystal jewels in flower patterns scattered throughout the fabric.

Excitement tingled through her body as she imagined the fancy date she was going on. She danced and spun around her apartment, thinking about Charlie.

They'd been dating for over a year and he'd said they were going to Gratzi Italiano for a special night out. He was the first person she'd dated who both her family and friends approved of. No one else had lasted long enough to even meet her parents before Charlie. Smart with a good job, he was more than she could believe. Her luck the day she'd run into him at the farmers' market still amazed her. And then agreeing to go out for pancakes. *Who asks for a pancake on a first date?!*

She slipped on her black heels and the matching black purse, then skipped to the front room and found her favorite shawl to wrap around her shoulders. Though she felt alight with jubilation for the evening, she wondered why he would ask her out to such an elegant restaurant. There could be only one reason – she'd spoken to her best friends Emma and Tucker about this – the restaurant, the rich clothes…the night had to end in a ring…right?

Jamie spun again, a bit nervous and giddy, just as her doorbell rang. She took a moment to breathe before she opened the door. Charlie stood there in a light gray suit, black shirt, and black tie. Her heart pounded in anticipation and she smiled, excited for the evening ahead of her.

He smiled back, sexy as always. He'd charmed her

with that smile when they'd met. "You look lovely, Jamie. Are you ready?"

"I am." She followed him to his silver Tesla, sliding in and enjoying the ride to downtown Chicago.

Once they arrived, they were led to a private table in an alcove with terracotta sconces and a candle in the center of the table. The maze through the other tables, full of couples in their elaborate clothes, talking quietly, amped her nerves. *There are so many people here, but the table is private and it almost feels like we're alone.* Her heart pounded harder. She tried to calm her nerves as she read over the menu, though the staccato beat didn't want to stop racing. She quickly decided on what she wanted and put the menu down.

"Do you know what you want?" She gazed up into his dark brown eyes expectantly. *I know what I want...you.* This had to be the night!

He placed his menu down, leaned back, and folded his hands in his lap. "Jamie, we need to talk." His face was held tight. This wasn't the look of love she'd expected.

Dread fought with the hope and elation she'd felt all evening. Her gut suddenly felt like it'd been filled with sawdust, and she tried to swallow, but her mouth was dry. "We do?"

"You know I love you; we've been doing this dating dance for over a year and I've thought long and hard about our future together...I just...Jamie, do you honestly love me back?"

His words felt like a punch to her ever twisting gut. Of course she loved him; how could he question her love and her heart? *Of course I love him…don't I?*

"How can you question me?" Her voice sounded raspy, thin and weak. This wasn't how she expected the evening to proceed. Wasn't she supposed to get a ring? A proposal? This was supposed to be the night her dreams came true. "I thought our lives would become one tonight." Her eyes burned and the words quietly slipped out.

He lifted his hand as if to reach for her, then shook his head and let it drop again. "I love you, but again, I think you need to figure things out. I often feel like you love me as a friend, a really good friend, but not more than that. I don't know that you feel the burning love I feel for you. Have you ever really thought about who you truly love? You know all I want is for you to be happy." He paused for a moment. "You seem distracted by women who walk by; did you know that? Maybe I'm wrong. I'm just saying, maybe we should take a couple of weeks apart to figure out our hearts before we make any lifelong decisions."

Body quaking and numb, Jamie couldn't believe what she heard. Her nails biting into her palms snapped her out of her frozen state enough that she slowly stood, spun on her heel, and walked from the restaurant. She heard Charlie calling for her, but knew she couldn't face him. Not after the accusations he'd thrown at her.

She jumped into the first cab she found, giving the driver her address. The ride was a blur she barely remembered, her body numb with despair. Once home, she kicked off her heels, poured a glass of wine, and dropped onto her couch, turning the TV on to find a sappy movie to distract her.

How dare he tell me what I want in life! I know what I want! I was ready to spend the rest of my life with him. How dare he say those things to me, think he knows me better than me, and to think he's *the one my family loved. Well, Mr. Tall, Dark, and Handsome doesn't know what he's just lost out on. I'm smart, and pretty. I work for an important company and I'm moving up. There are lots of men who would want to be with me. Charlie doesn't know what he's lost!*

Finishing off the wine in her glass, she started to pour another glass of wine before she hesitated and set the glass on the table and drank directly from the bottle. *But what if he's right?* A shiver of dread and something she didn't want to think about wound down her body. *What if this is the reason I've never really connected with all my boyfriends growing up? There was that time Cindy and I practiced kissing in college, but all girls do that, right? My heart had pounded faster than normal, but that didn't mean anything. And everyone is a bit in love with their best friends in high school... right? I just always thought that's what was expected of me. Could it be true?*

Do I like women?

CHAPTER 4

Anastasia sat on the floor in Malcolm's room and cried. Thinking about the day, she leaned back on his bed, hugged her knees to her chest, and rested her chin on her knees. The tears wouldn't stop. Malcolm and Adrian sat on the floor with her, eyes puffy from crying. They'd all gone to the official funeral earlier that morning. The death of the King, beloved by all, had shaken the land to its core. Everyone had come out to pay their respects. Now Anastasia just wanted to grieve in private for her pa…not for the King.

Adrian, face wet with tears, wiped his eyes. "What do you think will happen next? Can Mum run the country by herself?"

Malcolm nodded, stretched out his legs, and leaned back on his hands. "She can. She's smart and the two of them always discussed all the decisions. I'm sure she'll continue to run things for long enough for sis here to figure out her life…assuming you ever do, Star."

She huffed out a laugh and gave a small smile, the pain of her pa's death still a dagger in her heart. "I don't know if I ever will. Let's hope her reign as Queen is long and prosperous. I'm happy learning under her for many years to come, volunteering in town, and doing my charity work. I'm in no rush—"

"To marry?" Malcolm interrupted. "You have no young lad waiting in the wings to sweep you off your feet?"

"No, Malcolm; that's all you." Both Anastasia and Malcolm gaped at Adrian when he said that. She didn't know Adrian had seen Malcolm with any of his boyfriends and from Malcolm's face, he hadn't known either. Adrian almost fell over laughing. "If you two could see your faces! What, you think I'm too daft to notice what's right under my nose? Your dalliances are discrete, but not hidden. Our rooms *are* right across the hall from each other, and sneaking in and out of the window isn't *that* original."

Anastasia laughed. "I just can't believe you kept the secret, Adrian. Who knew it was possible? You've never kept anything secret before."

"I've kept plenty of things secret; you've just never known because of the front I put on of *not* keeping secrets. It's all been a ploy." His boyish smile almost made up for the times he'd gotten her in trouble with his tattling on her.

Malcolm stared at the ceiling, still shaking his head. "I can't believe you've known all this time and have never let on." He sat up and crossed his legs. He leaned in towards Adrian with a small smirk. "What other secrets do you know, little brother?"

Eyes alight with mischief, Adrian shook his head. "Oh, no. I'll not give anything else away. You two will just have to wonder what things I know that you've imagined you've expertly kept from me…but have you?" He raised one eyebrow in challenge. "Or am I sitting here knowing everything? I may have a spy network out there working to let me know everything happening in the palace."

Anastasia considered her brother. "A spy network? I'll have to remember that, when I'm to become queen. I'll need to know all these secrets. You're slated to be the head of finances and running the books of the kingdom, but you could do that and be spymaster…couldn't you?"

Before he could answer, a soft knock came at the door. Before any of them could react, Sidney, their mum's advisor now that their pa was gone, poked his head in. "Pardon me, Your Highnesses, but the Queen has asked that you all join her in the day room presently."

With a sniffle, Anastasia gave each of her brothers a hug before they stood and straightened their outfits. She had to switch her mindset from grieving daughter to Princess.

They headed down the main staircase to the dayroom, with a wall of windows to let in the light. Anastasia's fractured focus took in the couches, large terracotta vases with colorful flowers, and trays with pastries, before she hugged her mum and then sat in a chair facing the Queen. Her brothers hugged their mum as well before sitting and Sidney took a seat on the far side of the couch with their mum. Though Anastasia knew her mum grieved the loss of their pa, she held it in before the three of them.

Although she wasn't hungry, Anastasia selected a lemon macaron and ate the tart treat. She needed a bit of a delay before learning what their mum wanted from them. The sweet dessert coated her mouth, so she signaled a servant for coffee. She took a stabilizing breath, smiled, and said, "Mum, how are you holding up?"

Mum took a sip of tea, holding the saucer in her other hand. She carefully placed both back on the table, the two clattering together on the way down. After taking a minute to compose herself, her mum stared at her blankly. "My dearest Star." Mum rarely called her Star, insisting it was too informal. This wasn't good. "I know I can continue to rule this kingdom on my own, for a short time at least. Your father and I were a true partnership in all ways. The thing is, I don't want to. When I met your father and fell in love, agreeing to become the Queen of Ixica, I did it to be with him, not for the love of ruling. Over the years, I became proficient at what I do, but I'm tired. I will remain on the throne until you marry and take over, but at that point, I shall retire."

Ice formed in Anastasia's veins and she felt frozen to her chair. She barely noticed when the coffee was handed to her. The warmth seeped into her hands as she sat there holding the mug, mindlessly seeing nothing, not knowing what to say.

Sidney cleared his throat. "Princess Anastasia…" He paused as if embarrassed. Then his face hardened as he barreled on. "I assume you still have your signet ring. I've not seen it for years, but you used to wear it around your neck as a child. You'll need to wear it once you're Queen."

Chills ran down her spine, intensifying the cold infusing her soul. A memory of a girl with green eyes the color of moss that grew on stones. A smile that lit up her heart. Brown curls that bounced when the girl ran off ahead of her in a race that wasn't fair. Why wasn't it fair? Because Star didn't know the end point, that was it. Jamie had cheated! The autumn her family would learn about the United States by spending a week in the center of the country. A magical week when Anastasia met Jamie and promised to marry her.

She tried to repress the shiver and let out a breath. Anastasia looked at Malcolm, wondering if he'd overheard anything that day at the treehouse. After a moment to let her mind settle, she turned to Sidney. "My ring? Why haven't you seen it in a while? Well…"

Malcolm selected a small petit four. "She doesn't have it because she promised it to someone when she was twelve and we were visiting America. Anastasia is already engaged."

CHAPTER 5

The paper bag sat on the table next to the open bottle of wine. Emma had told Jamie exactly what she'd expected her to do as she'd left work that afternoon. *Take this bag, don't open it until you've had a glass of wine…and be ready to hit a club at eight. Tucker and I will be there to pick you up! No more sitting around your apartment in a stupor, girl.*

Jamie'd gotten home, showered, and found the perfect outfit. She held the empty wine glass and wondered what Emma had given her. She and Emma had been friends since she started at Moore Stone Industries. Since she started working as a project manager, she'd worked her way up steadily, proving her worth to the company. Emma and Tuckler had been working their way up through the ranks with her for the last three years, though Tucker was a shooting star already at the top, his ability in IT security was almost mythical.

Jamie placed her glass down next to the bottle and picked up the bag. Checking the time, she saw she had a half hour. Inside the bag she found a magazine with the words *Buxom Beauties* screaming back at her. Eyes wide, her hands loosened and the bag with its magazine slid from her grasp and dropped to the floor. Now, she knew what her friend had planned, she reached out with a shaking hand to refill her glass and gulp down more wine. Fortified, she grabbed the bag and pulled out the magazine.

On the cover was a brunette wearing very little with two fingers in her mouth. Big, puppy-dog eyes gazed into the camera as her bikini top barely covered anything. She leaned in towards the lens as if she wanted to look into the soul of every person holding the dirty rag.

Taking a shaky breath, Jamie started paging through the images one by one, chills racing up and down her spine, and her arms began to feel heavy and numb as she gazed at scantily-clad bodies on each page. Once she got to the end, she pushed the glossy pictures to the side and poured herself more wine. Body buzzing and mind whirling, she sat and waited until her doorbell rang. "It's open."

Emma and Tucker breezed in, taking in the scene in an instant. Emma tsked. "Oh honey, that outfit will never do. What *are* you wearing?"

Jamie's chin dropped as she let her eyes roam the black pencil skirt and white button down shirt she wore. "What? I look nice. You told me to dress nicely."

"I told you to dress to go to a club. You look like you're ready to take notes at a trial. Come on, let's find you something better."

Not sure she wanted to trust her friends, she got up and slowly followed them to the bedroom. Dizzy with the wine, and confused by the images swirling in her head, Jamie narrowed her eyes at the back of her friend's bouncing curls as they disappeared into her closet. "What's with that magazine, Emma?"

A laugh came from her closet as she dropped onto her bed next to Tucker. "I thought you should get inspired. If you're going to see if Charlie is right, you should really find out. Stop sulking, start figuring this all out. It's been over two weeks and you need to get out of this apartment. That's what we're here for."

Tucker sat cross legged on her bed holding the magazine. *When did he grab that? Maybe he'd grabbed it on the way in.* "Is this what women...or straight men find attractive? I mean, I get the artistic beauty of the female form, but this is awful."

With a huff, Jamie flopped to her stomach, trying to get the horrible magazine out of sight. "Get rid of that! Do you really think Charlie could be right? I thought I was happy with him for over a year. I expected a ring, not any of this! Am I really going to let him mansplain my own lovelife to me? This is ridiculous."

Tucker rubbed her back. "Oh, honey, he isn't mansplaining your life, he's just seeing something you weren't, and aren't, admitting to yourself. We just want to make sure you explore this before you commit to anything."

Before he got done talking, clothes Jamie barely recognized flew at her and fell onto the bed, preceding Emma out of her closet. Her fiery friend shook her head, red curls flying, and put her two cents in. "He isn't explaining you to you, he's protecting his heart. And, yeah, he may be right. We've known you since college, and though you've been subtle, personally, I've wondered on and off. Now put these on." She thrust an octopus print shirt and black mini skirt into Jamie's arms.

Rolling her eyes, Jamie slipped into the closet and slid on the clothes, then the plaid overshirt. "If you'd wondered, why not ever ask?"

Tucker snorted. "Honey, you can be prickly. Sometimes it's better to just wait things out."

She straightened her clothes, unhappy with her friends, but thinking about what they'd said. Once she had everything on, she presented her new outfit.

Emma smiled wide and declared them ready to go. She and Tucker dragged her out to a bar two blocks away with a sign on the door stating "ladies only on Wednesdays." Tucker raised a brow at the sign, "This is where I leave you ladies. Don't do anything I wouldn't, but since I'll do almost anything, that isn't very limiting! Have fun, my dears." He leaned over and gave Jamie and then Emma a kiss on the cheek.

Jamie engulfed him in a big hug. "Have fun tonight, Tucker."

His face lit with mischief. "Oh, I plan to!" And he headed down the street to execute his own plans.

She paused at the door knowing she delayed the inevitable. As she stood there, something niggled in the back or her mind, but then Emma dragged her into the bar, and it was gone.

Loud music assailed her as they fought their way across the bar through the crowd to order a drink. Emma got the bartender's attention and placed their order. Jamie found a table and watched the crush of people as they moved and danced around the small sectioned-off dance floor. Jamie wondered if she'd ever, in all her life, been attracted to a girl.

Emma dropped a glowing blueish green drink in front of her and raised an eyebrow, daring her to question it. Jamie sipped it and a sweet fruity flavor erupted in her mouth, and no alcoholic aftertaste. She knew she was in trouble with this drink.

Half-way through her drink, a tall blonde wearing a tight black halter dress approached as if she owned the place. She reached out a hand to Jamie, palm up, and demanded, "Dance."

Jamie froze and Emma kicked her under the table. "Of course she'll dance with you. Go, I'll watch your drink."

Carefully putting her drink down, Jamie let herself be led away. The two danced to a loud techno beat, their bodies gyrating together in the tight crowd on the dance floor. It was fun, but it felt like dancing with Emma or Tucker. At the end of the song, before Jamie could escape, the woman leaned down and caught her mouth in a demanding kiss. The woman continued to sway while they kissed, and Jamie was forced to grab the woman's hips, or fall.

Bracing herself she thought. *Now or never. I may as well give in to what everyone has been saying.* And she kissed the woman back, leaning in and letting her hands slide around to the woman's back.

Just like she predicted, she felt nothing. She didn't know why she was there, what she was doing, what Charlie had been going on about. In the back of her mind, she admitted she'd kissed some men with just as little reaction, but this woman, for all intents, was gorgeous, a blonde knock-out.

As quickly as she could, she peeled herself away from the woman and headed back towards the table. Another song started up, and a freckled brunette with spiky hair, bleached at the end, thick dark makeup, and a Ramones t-shirt, started dancing, rubbing their bodies together. Before Jamie knew what she was doing, the brunette grabbed her hips and spun her close.

The woman slid a hand around Jamie's waist and Jamie found her legs intertwining with the other woman's. Jamie's hands came up and wrapped around the stranger's neck, and her dance partner smiled as if in victory. The brunette leaned in, as if to ask a question and Jamie found herself in another kiss. This one tasted dark and dangerous.

The woman slid her tongue into Jamie's mouth and the world froze. The music stopped and the other people disappeared. Jamie's arms tightened as she pulled the other woman closer. She groaned when the kiss deepend and her body began to tingle in a way she hadn't felt since...

She broke away from the kiss, the music and the people coming back in a rush. Dizzy and confused, she wove her way back to the table to find Emma standing with a shit-eating grin on her face. Jamie shook her head. "This isn't the first time, Em. My first kiss. How could I forget, how could I forget Star?"

The bar was too hot, and she needed air. She gulped, breathing deeply, and spun on her heel. Jamie ran to the door, and the cool air hit her face, sending a chill down her spine. Her mind split between the present and the past as she walked towards her apartment. A need in her pushed her to run, but she didn't want to garner any extra attention. But the pull she felt to get home…she was determined to see if her memories were correct.

The sound of footsteps came from behind her… pounding on pavement. *That's not fair! I've never been here before!* Memories…black hair streaming behind jewel-like blue eyes…could it be? Her heart pounded in her chest and Jamie shot a look over her shoulder but instead of the dark-haired twelve-year-old, Emma chased her, concern etched in her green eyes…green, not blue.

Jamie slowed down to let her friend catch up. Emma held her hands against her ribs as she gulped in air. "Where are you going? What do you mean you forgot about the stars? Jamie, talk to me. You aren't making sense, you're scaring me. Was that drink too much?"

Jamie closed her eyes to focus on the here-and-now and slipped her arm into Emma's. Together they continued to her apartment. She explained on the way about a magical week in November when she'd met a girl who had enchanted her.

When they arrived at the apartment, Jamie searched her jewelry box, but knew the ring wouldn't be there. She wore jewelry enough to know everything in her collection. She dug into her closet until she got onto her hands and knees and found the boxes her parents had packed up for her after she'd graduated college. *We don't want your old junk anymore, Jamie. Take it or we toss it!*

With a bit of effort, she pulled them out. She and Emma started pawing through the trinkets of her past, books and pictures, school notes and knick knacks.

"Oh, my God, Jamie, look at the clothes you wore in high school! This is hilarious. I'm taking this and posting it on the work gossip site." Emma giggled.

Jamie groaned and reached for the picture. "No! That was for a school musical, and I was in the chorus. I wasn't even good enough for anything but the back row. Anyone who tried out was allowed some bit part and trust me, if they could, they would've kicked me out."

With a twinkle in her eyes, Emma tucked the picture into her purse and started to bounce. "This picture is gold, I tell you, gold!"

With only a couple boxes left, Jamie started to question her memories. Had she saved the ring? Could it be lost? At the bottom of one, she found a blue plastic trinket box. She searched her memories about what this box meant when she'd been younger and froze. Her heart pounded as she slowly pulled it out. The box was in the shape of a dragon with a ruby eye. Opening it, she found a silver chain holding a ring with a gold and silver woven band. The face of the ring had a stylized 'T' interwoven with vines and leaves. Her hands shook and her heart stopped as she gazed at the trinket she thought was only a memory. Had she hoped it wasn't real?

It's real. The promise ring. Star.

CHAPTER 6

The coffee wasn't enough to cut through the fog in Anastasia's brain. She'd spent the last week sitting in meeting after meeting with her mum and Sidney, beginning the transition that would allow her to be Queen of Ixica. She'd studied her whole life, yet this felt like more than everything she'd ever learned.

A plate of pastries and fruit slid in front of her as she ruminated on the ring she'd given away all those years ago. Did Jamie still have it? What would she do if the signet ring was lost? Would the crown automatically move to Malcolm? How badly would she let down her mother, her country, herself if the ring were never found? And if they do find Jamie, would there still be feelings between them? Did she remember her? As she ate, the rest of her family and Sidney joined her.

They ate in a small family room off the kitchen. Sidney wasn't family, but he was a friend and advisor and his invitation to the table was assumed, even when there wasn't business to discuss for the day. As he ate he eyed her, and that didn't bode well for her. She dug into her food, waiting for the bad news to come.

He leaned back in his chair, a small pastry in his hand, smiling in delight at the family all gathered together. "Now, Anastasia, have you made arrangements with this Jamie fella? Does he still agree to the proposal from when you were twelve? I imagine not...so long ago. Does he even remember you? Most importantly, can you get your ring back? Does he still have it?"

She groaned and finished off the last of her coffee, the light brown, creamy caffeine almost too sweet. As she drank, she saw Malcolm cover his mouth with his hand to hold back a laugh.

When a servant came to refill her mug, she quickly said, "Black this time." She faced Sidney and plastered on a smile. "Well, no. I'll need to fly out and find Jamie, talk with...um," she bit her lip and shook her head. "Discuss this matter face to face. I don't think this is something to be done from a distance, don't you agree? I'm sorry, it will just take a bit longer than initially expected."

Sidney's face tightened and he took a deep breath. "You can't fly to America alone, it isn't proper for a princess. I guess I could fly out there with you, if I must."

With a clang, Malcolm's mug hit the table. "Oh, you couldn't leave Mum, not a time like this. You are too crucial to the country, and our family. I can clear my schedule and head out with her. My job has...well, it has seemed to have opened up for the next few weeks, so why don't I act as escort?"

Adrian finished off the last of his breakfast, searching for a server to get him a new plate of food. "Don't you need to head back to work? You've only just started working in your consulting job. How can you take off? Please don't tell me you're going to play the royal family card. That's just so...gah! Just don't! I can go. I work for the family doing finances. I really can take the time, work remotely."

Mum slowly ate her pancakes. With a small smile, she put down her tea and leaned back. "Adrian, dear, do you not know that Malcolm works with Casimir as a fashion designer?"

If the floor opened up and she dropped into a pit, she'd be less surprised. Anastasia gaped at Mum. Malcolm had the same astonished look on his face.

With a wink, she continued. "I assume with the upcoming nuptials, he doesn't want you involved? There *is* something gauche about working on your sister's wedding, don't you think?"

Malcolm's mouth opened and closed a few times before, nodding, he finally got some words out. "How did you know? How *long* have you known?"

"Well, I think I've always known you've enjoyed fashion. As for working with Casimir," she said shrugging, "I guess when you started to be happy to go to work. He's the only fashion designer in Ixica, so I questioned him. He told me the truth."

Shrinking into himself, voice small, Malcolm asked, "Did Pa know?"

With a small sigh, Mum deflated a bit. "No. He wouldn't have understood letting you grow to be the man *you* wanted to be. I loved him with all my heart, but he had plans for all of you and wanted you to be the man *he* wanted. I was going to begin working on him once I'd confirmed what you did… but I didn't have time. I know, given time, he would've come to accept everything there is about you. So, yes, you should escort Anastasia to get her ring, and maybe her Jamie."

Ready for the conversation to be over, Anastasia stood. "Well, I'm off to check on the arrangements and start packing. It's been a delight."

Before she took more than a couple steps, Sidney stopped her. "You have a meeting with Casimir at ten. He'd like to start planning out the wedding and needs to get some initial direction from you. Don't be late."

Before meeting Casimir in the ballroom, Anastasia found the respite she needed in the garden. The gardeners had the ability to make the flowers bloom even in the worst weather conditions. The paths cut through roses of different colors. She sat at her favorite bench facing orange and yellow blooms. They reminded her of sitting with her pa and discussing any issue they may have. A few minutes here and she felt she could face an army...possibly even Casimir.

Once she found him, he had boards set up with ideas: fabrics, dresses, colors, flowers, and more questions than Anastasia could answer. Head spinning, she turned in place, taking in the hundreds of images of smiling couples in white and black, flowers of all shades, attendees behind them shining like jewels. Head swimming, she found a couch to fall into. Only after the servant brought her a glass of water did she realize she'd landed on a fainting couch. *Ironic...*

"Oh, my lovely Anastasia, are you okay? I know this wedding is going to be fabulous, my crowning jewel as a designer. Together, we'll present you—the new Queen—to the world." He stood over her in his immaculate black slacks, a skin-tight top featuring a print of an oversized gold crown, and a white button-down shirt, open and untucked. His brown wavy hair just touched his shoulders, the same color as his sparkling brown eyes.

She took a sip of water and then stood. "We're planning a wedding when I'm the only one in the engagement party. I don't know how fabulous that is, Casimir. But, yeah, let's make some decisions, though who knows; maybe my partner will want to change everything."

"Oh! You royals and your crazy backward ways. You make me glad I'm single, and remind me why I want to stay that way. Marriage, can you imagine? Well, I guess that's exactly what you're doing…"

His enthusiasm finally broke through her brooding and made her laugh. "You're renowned as both a clothes designer and a wedding planner, yet you've never wanted to get married?"

He threw his head back and roared. "Not in my life, never. I've seen how crazy a wedding is, and often the after effects of the marriage. I work with married couples all the time, and not many of them seem happy. Now, me, I'm happy." He dragged her over to the first board. "We have lots of decisions to make. Since you're taking my favorite assistant to America, we've got our work cut out for us. Let's start narrowing down our choices."

Later that night, Anastasia began sorting through everything she'd bring with her on her trip. It hadn't taken Finley long to find Jamie, computer wiz that he was. She stared at the itinerary, her gaze resting on the word 'Chicago' and thought about the small town in Wisconsin from her past. Disregarding her need to pack, she sat on the edge of her bed and pulled up a map of Chicago and the surrounding area. Wisconsin was just north of the big city. She'd enjoyed the visit to the quiet state when she was young, but the idea of visiting such a tourist trap now excited her. *Maybe Malcolm and I can take in some of the sights, become tourists for a couple of days. It may be good for both of us to leave our responsibilities behind.*

Opening the weather app on her phone, she entered "Chicago, Illinois, USA," and checked what the temperature would be for the next week or so. Their weather was similar to Ixica's, so she didn't have to pack a winter coat or boots.

A knock on her door was the only warning before Malcolm barged in. He never was one for waiting to be invited in anywhere; she was a bit surprised he'd even knocked. He crossed to her bed and flopped down. "So, Mum figured out one of my secrets. When will you tell her about Jamie?"

Anastasia laughed and shook her head. "How about never. We're going to go find this woman, tell her our story. Hopefully she'll still have the ring and we can get it back, and we'll come home. Do you think, in a million years, an

American woman will drop everything and return to Ixica with us? I'm just glad Mum doesn't remember who Jamie is."

"And what if Jamie decides to go for it; return and marry you?"

Hope surged in Anastasia, shocking her with its intensity. *She stared into the large green eyes and couldn't fathom why this wondrous girl said yes, she could kiss her.* She swallowed it before Malcolm noticed and gave a quick shake of her head. "No, not possible. She probably doesn't even remember me. How could she want to marry some random stranger from her past? God, she would have to leave her life, fly to Europe, and marry a stranger..." Her voice had gotten quieter with each point. She started to feel overwhelmed with the enormity of the task ahead of them. There was no way this would work.

Malcolm sat up and grabbed her hands, eyes narrowing shrewdly. "Look, Star, don't give up before we get there. You don't know who Jamie has turned into. But, if she's become half the woman you think she is, who better to bring her home to Ixica than the two of us?"

A new feeling of excitement bubbled in her at his words. She smiled and nodded, then shooed Malcolm from her room, and got back to packing.

CHAPTER 7

Jamie sat in her office, gazing out the window and envisioning Lake Michigan. All she saw from her window were the buildings across the street from Moore Stone Industries. The sun shone across her oak desk, organized with the piles of work she needed to finish this week. With a sigh, she leaned back, letting her head fall to her chair to stare at the ceiling. "How many floors up would I need to be promoted to see the lake? Four floors? Seven?"

"Nine."

With a start, Jamie sat up to see Emma leaning against her door frame. Emma's hair somehow stayed contained in clips so the curls cascaded down her back. She wore a cream pants suit over an eggplant button down shirt. Jamie smiled wide and straightened in her chair. "Floor nine, or nine floors up?"

Emma pushed off and came in to sit across from her at her desk. "If you'd just apply for the promotion I told you about last week, it wouldn't matter. You'd be doing what you went to school for, and I could visit you up in la-la land."

At Emma's words, she slumped. "The application was due last week to HR. They are looking at both internal and external applicants. According to my resources, they have seventeen applicants right now, so anyone applying has to be excellent."

The more Jamie detailed the facts, the wider Emma's smile got. "You applied, didn't you? You wouldn't have gotten all the details if you hadn't."

"I did. Now, I'm going to get a coffee from the street vendor. I have my interview in an hour. Maybe nine floors up has good coffee, but this floor doesn't. We should ask Tucker when we see him next."

Emma's eyes twinkled with delight as she pushed up to her feet. "No wonder you wore your best suit!" Her lower lip pushed out in a fake pout. "I'm hurt you didn't tell me, but excited. They have to select you—you're perfect for the position. I wish I could head down for coffee with you, but there's my regular meeting in five. Now, if I were to find a mocha cappuccino on my desk *after* my meeting, I wouldn't be at all upset."

Jamie swung her purse over her shoulder and made her way to the elevator down to the street level. The ride was quick and she was happy to find no line at the coffee truck. She came down to the truck a few times a week, and the owner knew her by sight. As she walked up, he said, "House blend with a splash of milk?"

She closed her eyes and lifted her head to the clouds enjoying the warm sun and slight breeze. She gave the man a bright smile. "That would be lovely, thank you."

An accented voice came from behind her. "It's a good thing you added the milk, I've heard people who drink black coffee are psychotic."

With a laugh, Jamie turned to see a tall man with short black curly hair, his coppery skin glowed in the sun, and his blue eyes danced at her as he approached the front of the line to order his own coffee.

Narrowing her eyes at him—something about him seemed familiar—she handed over her money and took her paper mug. "Oh, I like black coffee, I just have the milk added here to hide my secrets."

With a conspiratorial wink, she walked to a bench, where she hoped to enjoy a few minutes of peace and quiet. Watching people Scurry back and forth in their fancy attire was one of her favorite pastimes. It had been a couple weeks since Charlie had broken up with her, and she debated calling him. Did she love him? She thought she did but every time she went to call, something inside stopped her. She did love him, but was she *in* love with him? She'd had the one night out with Emma where she'd kissed that woman, but the only thing she'd felt was confusion.

The kiss had brought back a memory, and as much as she'd tried to dissect every bit of the memory, it had been years ago and it felt hidden behind a cloud of mist she couldn't penetrate. She'd called home, but her parents hadn't been much help.

"Where did you go? You're a million miles away."

The man with the accented voice had sat next to her, and she hadn't even noticed. "Are you following me?" She smiled, the niggling feeling she knew him had returned.

A soft laugh. "So suspicious. No…well, maybe. I think I know you, and maybe you know me. You wouldn't happen to be Jamie Woods?"

His hand reached out and stopped her coffee from falling as her hand and jaw slackened. "How? But? Huh?"

"My name is Malcolm. We met years ago. You and my sister were inseparable for that week when you were girls." He gave her coffee back.

Jamie couldn't get air. *Can this really be happening? I just thought of Star for the first time last weekend, she's taken over my thoughts, and now her brother appears? Can that be real?*

She inhaled sharply and whispered, "Star."

Her world tilted on its axis as he smiled wide. "You do remember us; fantastic! Anastasia will be thrilled."

Still uncertain whether she could breathe, she watched as he waved at a black Bently idling by the side of the road. A woman stepped out with the same black hair and copper skin. Her hair cascaded down her back in waves dark as night. She wore a dress blue as a summer's sky, matching the sparkle in her eyes. She sauntered over to them with a smile on her face.

As she drew closer, the memory piqued in Jamie. She licked her lips as she tipped her head, looking at the vision of beauty approaching. Superimposed was a memory of a girl running through the woods in dirty jeans and a t-shirt. *That was not fair!* Though she gazed at an elegant woman, the face held the echo of someone young and playful, a friend from the past.

Jamie held her coffee in her cold hands, letting the warmth seep into her. She bit her lower lip, words breathy with uncertainty she said, "Star…er Anastasia?"

The woman's eyes widened and her smile grew. "You remember?"

Voice trembling, Jamie nodded slowly as she spoke. "I do. I was recently reminded of your visit all those years ago. It's like that memory brought you…why did you return? How did you find me?"

Malcolm bumped shoulders with her. "It took a bit of research, but you do know you're on the internet, right? Once we found you, it didn't take long to find where you work. I wanted some coffee, and when I saw you, I thought I recognized the older version of the girl we'd met. If you'd not been you, we would've kept looking."

Jamie snorted, then glanced back and forth between them. "Just gone up to every brown-haired girl and said, 'Are you Jamie Woods?' until one of them blanched? Dropped right there in front of you in pure shock? Maybe sprayed you with pepper spray?"

"Oh, I like her, we should keep her!" Malcolm said, shifting his focus to Star.

Star paused, narrowing her eyes at her brother. "Right." After a beat, her face softened and her gaze went back to Jamie. "Jamie, we were, well, I was hoping to talk to you. Are you by any chance available to talk?"

Shivers of anticipation danced to her belly. Jamie wanted to say yes, but knew she had an important meeting that afternoon...soon even. Staring into the blue depths of Star's eyes and feeling she could get lost, she opened her mouth to answer, and forgot what she needed to say. She closed her eyes and took a breath, trying to center her thoughts. "I can't right now, but maybe tonight? I could meet you at seven?"

She refocused on Star in time to see her glorious smile

which hit her like a punch to the gut. Star agreed, and they swapped numbers. They would pick Jamie up at her place.

Jamie realized she'd do anything for another one of Star's smiles. She had to get away from this pair before she agreed to something she couldn't do. Before she returned to the office building, she remembered to get Emma her coffee. She saw the brother and sister slip into their car and drive away. As she entered the door, the air conditioning hit her hard.

She punched the button for the elevator, her mind a million miles away. She shook her head. Interview, she needed to focus on her interview.

Why do I feel like my life has just taken a turn into the unknown?

CHAPTER 8

Anastasia paced their hotel suite. Bedroom, living room, sitting room, patio, sitting room, Malcolm's room, and back. She continued to circle the rooms, her hands numb as her mind tumbled through the possible outcomes of the evening. Like the pacing, her emotions circled. She felt by turns elated, then terrified, then hopeful. She continued to walk, her heels clacking on the marble floor.

Malcolm slammed his book shut. "For the love of Pete, would you just sit? You've been all over this place for the last hour, and you're driving me batty. Tonight will be fine. I'll drive you and the lovely Jamie to dinner, sit at the bar, and let you discuss your hopes and dreams. Now…sit!"

She paused and glared at him. "Fine, I'll sit. But Malcolm, we're asking her to leave a life she's built here. I'm pretty sure she'll just laugh in our faces…my face. How can a person even consider leaving their life in such a bizarre scenario? And the idea she still has the ring." She collapsed into the chair, burying her face in her hands. "This is a fool's errand. We should've mentioned the ring this afternoon. Maybe she could've looked for it before we pick her up."

Malcolm leaned back on the couch and sighed. "Why don't we get in the car now and take a tour of this city. We could do the gangster tour, or just see as many of the Chicago sights as we can before picking up Jamie in a couple of hours. You need a distraction."

With a gusty release of air, Anastasia had to admit he was right. "Okay, fine, let's go. Let me find my purse."

Chicago traffic being as thick and insane as rumors predicted, they didn't actually get to see much of the city. A picture with The Bean, a bit of shopping on the Magnificent Mile, and then the slow inching north to Lincoln Park, Jamie's neighborhood.

"I'm never going to find parking. Why don't I drop you off and you go and meet her. I'll circle the block and pick you up." Malcolm's voice stayed calm despite the frustration she saw in the way he held the steering wheel.

"I'll try to be quick in getting her out to where you're

waiting." She leapt from the car and found the brick walkup that looked straight from a movie. The wrought iron banister slid under her hand as she ascended. She searched the names until she found 'Woods' and pressed the button.

It only took a few moments before Jamie's voice came over the speaker, a bit tinny. "I'll be down in a minute."

Excitement surged through Anastasia, mixed with a bit of disappointment. She'd hoped to see where Jamie lived. However, it would be better to save Malcolm from driving in circles. As she waited, she gazed up and down the street, noticing the buildings with their manicured lawns trapped behind gates. There were a few stores boasting different wares. She wondered if the brunch shop at the corner was any good.

An image flitted through her mind, of waking up with Jamie and walking to the corner to break their fast. Lost in her own world she missed when the real person approached her from behind. "Hi, Star…oh, is that what I should even call you anymore?"

Anastasia turned fast enough that she almost lost her balance and slid down the stairs. She didn't fall because of Jamie's quick catch of her arm. She gaped at Jamie's shocked wide eyes.

Jamie wore a mauve silk sleeveless dress that only went over one arm. It started off loose at the top, her necklace lost under the neckline. The dress then hugged her curves, flaring out into a skirt that ended just above her knees. She'd done her hair up and applied smokey-eyed makeup. Anastasia's heart began to pound faster just taking it all in. *God above I need to control myself, I'm losing myself for a woman who'll run once she hears what I have to say.*

Anastasia realized Jamie still waited for an answer. She tried to think back to what the woman had said, but had trouble piecing it all together. Finally she got her brain working. "You can call me Star, or Anastasia; either is fine."

A dazzling smile from Jamie nearly had her on her bum and her brain short-circuiting again. Jamie said, "Okay, well, I think I'll stick with Star for now, it's what I remember." Her head swiveled. "Where's Malcolm...and the car?"

As if on cue, the Bently pulled up, double parking near them on the street. Anastasia held out her arm and Jamie gently placed her hand on her elbow. Together, they descended the stairs.

Ignoring the other cars, Malcolm slipped out and opened the back door for them.

A man in a Toyota honked as he whipped his car around them. He yelled out his window, "Gargle my nuts you two-bit idiot!" And then, he drove off.

"Lovely," Malcolm groaned under his breath as Anastasia followed Jamie into the car. Anastasia bit back a laugh as the door closed behind them. Malcolm slid behind the wheel and took off toward the restaurant.

The Bently accelerated to the chorus of honks from the cars behind them. Jamie grabbed the back of the driver's seat with both her hands and leaned forward. "Do you actually know how to drive in this country? Do you have a license? Would you rather I drive?"

With a low chuckle, Malcolm turned towards downtown and the restaurant. "Do you think they'd rent a car to me if I wasn't legal to drive?"

Jamie's brow shot up. "That only counts if you really did rent this car. It doesn't look like a rental." She narrowed her eyes. "So, can you drive legally here?"

Anastasia placing a hand on Jamie's shoulder. "Why don't we let Malcolm drive, and we can talk. Maybe pretend he isn't here?"

The suspicion didn't leave her gaze as Jamie slowly slid back, letting her arms drop from the driver's seat. "Yeah, okay. This is a really nice car, by the way. Where are we going for dinner?"

Anastasia's shoulders dropped and she took a calming breath. She wanted Jamie to be relaxed and happy so she gave her a smile, hoping she'd approve of the cuisine choice. "I thought we could head to a Mexican restaurant, if that's okay with you."

The leather squeaked as Jamie adjusted to face her. "I'm good with anything, in general—I just like food."

"Then this is perfect. There really aren't many Mexican

restaurants in our country, not like what you have here."

Jamie's face softened. "Oh! I hadn't thought about that, but it makes sense. Mexican sounds perfect." She was silent for a few seconds before blurting. "Was there a specific reason you found me? It seems so weird you'd come looking for me after fourteen years. I mean, I can't think of any reason you'd come find me in person and not just call, or email, or something."

A tightness in Anastasia's gut distracted her. She tried to sort her thoughts to explain to Jamie exactly what they were doing, but dread overwhelmed her. Just as she opened her mouth to answer, the car lurched to a halt outside a loud, colorful restaurant. Her words scattered as she got out of the car. "I guess we're here," she said numbly, hoping she'd figure out a proper way to explain herself once they were seated.

CHAPTER 9

Jamie watched as Malcolm headed for the bar, not joining her and Star for dinner. Doubt soured her stomach as she followed the hostess, hoping she didn't act like a complete fool during the meal. *What's the worst that could happen? If I do act like an idiot, at least I don't have to worry about running into Star again after tonight. Just breathe, Jamie; just breathe.*

The fact she was with the most beautiful woman in the place made Jamie's breath catch. Suddenly Charlie's accusation made sense to her.

The waitress led them to a table by the window set

for two. Jamie slipped into the seat facing the door as the waitress poured them each a glass of ice water. "Can I get you anything to drink?"

Anastasia stared at Jamie, as if waiting for her suggestion. With all the tension she felt, Jamie smiled up at the waitress and nodded. "We'll each have a strawberry margarita. Maybe bring a pitcher."

She gave them a bubbly smile and said, "That's perfect. We have the best in town. Those will be right up and I'll give you a few minutes with the menu."

The music in the restaurant blared over the speakers, but not as loud as it played outside. Jamie figured she could hear the other tables conversations if she strained, but not easily. She tried to relax as she picked up her menu and looked over the names of food she'd been eating her whole life. It was something small, but it centered her, giving her some calm. "Do you have any questions?"

Across from her, Star took a sharp breath of air. "I thought we'd order first."

Jamie chuckled. "I meant about the menu and food options."

Eyes wide, Star smiled back. "Oh, would you like to order for both of us...like with the drinks? I don't know much about this cuisine."

"Ah...sure, I guess." She looked down at the menu, not really seeing the words. "Is there anything I should know about what you like or do not like?"

"No, I like everything."

This is a one night deal, just relax, Jamie. Have fun. We used to have fun together, remember the fun we used to have. "How about guacamole and chips for an appetizer, maybe chivice? For the main course, would you like fajitas? You can build your own. A burrito? Enchiladas? Mole? Something familiar? Tacos? Something fried, like a chimichanga? There are so many choices. Dessert is easy—Flan and tres leches…shared of course." Her stomach grumbled as she thought about all her options.

Star looked up from her menu. "You aren't very good at ordering for someone else, are you? You've mentioned just about everything on the menu. I like the starter and dessert. If we can get through what I want to ask you before the main meal comes, we can order enough for us and Malcolm, and he can join us. I like the fajitas and chimichurri. If Malcolm is joining us, a plate of tacos, they're his favorite. I'll quickly text him to let him know." She grabbed her phone from a slim, black purse and after a few moments put it back.

I love being on this date with Star, but leaving Malcolm alone in the bar seems unfair. I would love to have this dinner with her alone, but maybe having him here will make my stomach stop flipping.

The waitress returned with their drinks and Jamie put in their order. Star licked her lips and wrung her hands before forcing them down to her lap. "Do you remember when we were kids and I gave you my promise ring?"

It felt like all the air suddenly was forced from her body and the restaurant. Jamie rubbed her chest, trying to remember how to breathe, and felt the ring hidden in the folds of the top of her dress. "Yeah, I do. I was recently reminded of that night while talking to a friend."

"Well, in my country, Ixica, the giving of that ring is a promise. I know this sounds crazy, but it's equal to an engagement."

Jamie's hand fell, hitting the table. Before she could respond, she took a large gulp of her margarita, letting the cool, sweet alcohol fill her wobbly belly. "Are you saying we've been engaged...to be married...for fourteen years?" *Did my voice just go up an octave?*

Star winced, either at her words or pitch, she wasn't sure. "Well...yes. And that the holder of that ring should join me in ruling Ixica."

Jamie's hand shot out to grab her glass, and she took another swig of margarita, needing the strength. Voice reedy, she asked, "Are you here to ask for it back? I'm guessing you found someone better to help you run that country of yours. I can't imagine you'd still be interested in me. Not to mention, we barely even know each other...we're strangers."

There was a pause as Star just gazed at her across the table. Her dazzling blue eyes searched Jamie's face as if trying to find some answer. Finally, she closed her eyes and took a deep breath, letting it out slowly. Once she opened them again, she had the look of someone resolved in her decision. "Actually, no. I hoped I could convince you to return to Ixica with me for a couple of weeks to see if there was something to that engagement we made. Ixican engagements are not to be taken lightly…and I remember really liking you, Jamie Woods. I know you have a life here, but maybe if you spent some time in my world…I don't know, maybe you'd realize you like me, and Ixica, too."

A numbness flowed over Jamie as she sat gazing at the elegant beauty sitting across from her. *I'm engaged? I'm engaged to Star…to Anastasia…to Princess Anastasia, future Queen of Ixica?*

What about her job? The interview had gone well, but she'd been the first, and they wouldn't be making any decisions for a few weeks. She had plenty of vacation time.

Can I take two weeks off and travel to Ixica to meet the woman I've been engaged to for half my life? Does this type of thing really happen? Who has this life?

The waitress returned with their appetizer and she grabbed a chip and dipped it in the guacamole. What possible reason could there be to leave her life and traipse to the other side of the world? *What reason was there not to?* The debate happening in her head was intense.

She ate her third chip, then stared up into the sapphire blue eyes focused intently back on her, and couldn't imagine saying anything but 'yes' to this enchantress.

Before she could answer, Star gave a small smile. "How about you think about what I've asked, and I'll invite Malcolm over. We'll enjoy dinner, and you can tell me on the way back to your place."

"Okay, that sounds good." She'd pretty much decided, but having time to contemplate her decision was probably a good thing. She shouldn't leap into this too quickly.

Malcolm joined them, dragging a chair from an empty table nearby. He carried his drink from the bar, and smiled as he sat. "So, the two of you had enough time to discuss everything?" He faced Star. "Does she have the ring?"

Star blanched as they both faced her. Hand at her throat, Jamie looked back and forth between them as Star said, "I hadn't gotten around to asking about that yet."

Jamie swallowed past the lump in her throat, and slowly pulled out the ring, dangling on the same silver chain Star had looped around her neck all those years before. "I found it. I… uh…remembered it a few days ago and went looking for it. I, um, don't really know what possessed me to wear it tonight. I guess I thought I could give it back to you…if you want it."

Malcolm's eyes had grown to the size of saucers. "I can't believe you have the ring. That's brilliant! Have you also agreed to return to Ixica with us?"

Star voice sounded strained as she said, "We'll give her time to think about it." At the same time Jamie whispered, "Yes."

CHAPTER 10

"Your Highnesses, we'll be landing in forty minutes." The pilot spoke over the speaker, his large headphones covering his ears.

Anastasia put down her book, the latest by Parker Love, one of her favorite authors, and laid it on her crossed legs. She looked at Jamie curled up on the cream couch across from her. She slid the book to the cushions and stood, crossing the small distance. Malcolm sat in a bucket seat a bit down the plane. "Are you going to wake her up now?"

"I think so. That way she can see Ixica from up here and the landing. Give her some time to wake up before we disembark."

He shrugged. "That makes sense."

The plane bumped and Anastasia braced herself on the back of a chair that faced the rear of the plane. Another jerk, and she landed on Jamie's feet. Jamie shot up, eyes wide in confusion before she slumped. "Everything okay? Are we there? Have we landed?"

"The only landing was me on your feet, sorry about that." Anastasia scrunched up her face as heat rose to her cheeks.

Jamie curled her legs under her and laughed. "That's okay. Was it an accident, or were you waking me up for something?"

"A bit of both. We're about to land and I thought you'd enjoy seeing Ixica from the sky. But, I hadn't planned on landing *on* you to wake you. Once we're on the ground, the fun really begins."

Jamie's eyes widened as if Anastasia's words had been a threat. "What should I expect when we land? Does everyone know you're bringing me home? Will there be some sort of international incident?"

A soft chuckle came from the back of the plane. "Probably. But we need a good incident every few years to shake the people up. We wouldn't want our country to be boring, now, would we?"

Jamie darted a glance towards Malcolm, looking pensive, before her face blossomed into a huge smile, stilling Anastasia's heart. She forgot to breathe for a few moments, lost in the sight of Jamie's beauty.

Climbing to her knees, Jamie's eyes danced as she shared the joke with Malcolm. "I'm sure my entering Ixica amidst mystery and intrigue will be the proper and accepted way to introduce a new friend of the royal family. It must be how you present all your new…God, I don't even know what I am, person? I am your new person!"

Malcolm snorted. "That you are, m'lady, the new person of the royals. I'll be sure when asked to say that is your official title. Person Jamie of America."

With a smile, she fell back, staring up at Anastasia. She wiggled her eyebrows before flipping around and pushing her nose to the window. "Is that Ixica?"

Anastasia knelt next to Jamie. "Over there, in the distance, you can just see Fridon, the main city. You can just make out the city lights."

"Please put on your belt, we are preparing for landing." Following the pilots directions, both women twisted around, got up, and moved to the bucket seats to buckle in.

The landing was smooth, and before long they were back on solid ground. Anastasia led them to a limo that would take them home. As she reached for the door, Jamie shuffled to a stop behind her. "What about our bags?" Her head fell back as she gazed up at the sky, rotated in place, then searched the airport at large.

Malcolm huffed out a laugh as the driver got the door.

People on the sidewalk began to take notice of them so Anastasia put her hand on Jamie's arm to stop her motion. "The bags will be brought for us; we just need to get in the car. Malcolm will direct the driver to take the long way, giving you a quick tour of the land."

Once they managed to get Jamie into the car, Malcolm poured drinks, and the driver began the tour.

The seats in the back of the limo faced in three directions. Anastasia and Jamie sat in the bench seat that faced forward. Malcolm took the seat perpendicular to them facing the door out. He stretched out his legs and sipped his wine. "We landed in the airport, which is located in the south eastern part of the city. The main city, Fridon, takes up most of the lower third of the country. Our palace is in the center, but it's in the northern part of the city with our own private land north and east."

The limo navigated the streets of Fridon, passing businesses and stores, a school, and homes near a park. There were people on the sidewalk going about their day, ignoring the limo as Jamie sat, face plastered to the window, wine forgotten, taking everything in.

Once they passed out of the city to the northwest, they crossed over the Banrick River and everything shifted from big city to provincial. Jamie, eyes wide with wonder, pivoted. "Are we still in Fridon? Ixica?"

Anastasia placed a hand on Jamie's leg. "Yes, we crossed

the Banrick River. This is Lomhal, a smaller town. They have a farmer's market every Saturday. They make a lot of items by hand here; it's rather lovely. There's a forest north of here. Across the river is our home and then a mountainous area. There's a lot of skiing and rock climbing in the mountains, if you like those activities."

The driver swung around and headed back towards the Palace. The limo took an older, less used bridge over the river. Jamie smiled as she said, "Are we really going over an old stone bridge that looks like it's from a fantasy book? Is this for real? And…safe?"

Both Anastasia and Malcolm laughed. A warmth of happiness at sharing her country with Jamie bubbled in Anastasia as she saw the wonder in the woman's face. She let her hand slip from Jamie's leg to her hand, and she gave it a squeeze. "It's safe, don't worry. We'll be at the house soon."

The limo made its way to the front of the palace, driving up the long driveway, and around the circular drive. They parked in front of the palace. As the engine turned off, and the driver opened the door, the front door of their home flew open, and Adrian ran out. Behind him, their mum and Sidney slowly exited the house, standing just outside the door, watching the three get out and stretch.

As the driver first helped Malcolm, then Anastasia out, the tension from the family ratcheted up. When Jamie stepped from the car, Adrian's mouth dropped open in an excited smile. "I knew it! I knew my memory wasn't wrong." He leapt forward, engulfing her in a hug that shocked everyone, by the stunned looks on their faces.

From the house, Sidney's voice shot out. "Anastasia, I believe we need to talk…alone."

CHAPTER 11

S tanding outside the limo with her glass of wine, Jamie watched as all the color drained from Star's face.

The youngest brother…the one who'd hugged her, smiled. "Why don't I show Jamie around while you go talk to Mum and Sidney." He slid his arm into hers before anyone could agree or protest. Malcolm grabbed her glass as her drink threatened to spill.

Eyes wide, Star nodded. "Yeah, okay Adrian, sounds good. See you back in the house in an hour?" Though she agreed, Star didn't sound happy.

The spit-fire of a young man had already dragged Jamie

to the edge of the house before yelling over his shoulder. "Sounds good!"

Jamie searched her memory, trying to remember Star's youngest brother. He would've been eight or nine, then. God, he'd seemed so much younger than their very mature twelve. "So, you're not eight anymore? Nine was it? How old were you back then…and now for that matter…not that it matters, I guess…" She could've hit herself. She sounded like a babbling idiot. Must be the jet lag. Oh God, where was she and why had she agreed to this trip.

"Well, that depends on who you ask. I may *act* like I'm still nine—it was nine by the way—but no, alas, I had to grow up like everyone else…start adulting." He sounded like growing up was an offense against him…maybe all humanity. "I'm now a ripe old twenty-three, if you must know."

Adrian came to a stop before they got to the edge of the long side of the building. "So, this is our home, but it's also the royale palace. We just left the main entrance, but there are a few other places to sneak in."

Jamie gazed up at the cream colored side of the home with circular corners and arched window bays. The roof glinted a dark blue in the setting sun. It looked like there were four or five stories and she couldn't imagine knowing her way around the imposing structure. "You live here? Home sweet home?" She squinted to estimate how far down the building stretched and the number of windows. "How cozy."

He snorted. "Yeah, the living area is separated on the far end and is a bit less…intimidating, I guess." He paused and considered. "You came in over there along the circular drive. South of the drive, about a mile from us, is the city." He continued walking around the palace. "If we continued this way, we'd wander the gardens and eventually get to a forest with wonderful walking paths. Maybe we can head out there tomorrow. You'll probably appreciate some down time by then."

She raised a brow at him. "What, you think all this will overwhelm me?"

With a laugh, he tugged her to the left. "Like I said, the far side is what we call home, this side is more business. As we come around the back, you see this." He waved his arm out like a game show host.

The back of the palace had a full glass room big enough to hold thousands of people. The setting sun shone in the room and she could see a wood floor with an inlay pattern. In the far corner were a few tables with what looked like grade-school science fair poster board. Narrowing her eyes she tried to see what was being presented, but she couldn't tell what it was. "Is there a science fair happening in there?"

Adrian smiled at her, his blue eyes—so like his sister's—danced with amusement. "Not that I couldn't see Anastasia arranging something like that, but no, not this time. This is something much more…well, I'll let my sister fill you in on what that is. Let's move on. This path takes us between the vegetable garden and the rose garden out to the stables. Do you know how to ride?"

She didn't know where to look first. The flowers were amazing, and the roses were blooming in several different colors, from red to orange, yellow to white. The food garden was lush, and Jamie wanted to pluck a tomato to eat. She realized she gaped at everything and slowly replayed what had been asked. "No, I mean, not really. I've been on a horse, but not since I was a kid. It's been ages."

"I bet you'd do fine, we have some docile animals."

The path opened up to a large field. At the far end was a huge stable with a fenced in pasture. Jamie saw several horses milling about, a black horse with a white snout, a white horse with black spots, a roan mare prancing around, ears lifted as if they were having fun. There were others grazing and just being beautiful.

Jamie realized she stood transfixed watching the animals. Adrian's chuckle brought her back as she shook herself. "They're amazing."

"I'm glad you think so. Like I said, maybe tomorrow we can go out in the forest, on the horses, and decompress from whatever bad news Sidney has to share with us *this* time."

Jamie rubbed her temples. "Sidney was the man with the woman at the door. Do you call your dad, the ah… King, um…Sidney or were they not your parents?"

The mirth drained from Adrian's face as he took a steadying breath. "Sidney isn't our father, though the woman was our mum. Our father died a few weeks back."

Cold dread shot through Jamie at how she misspoke. "I'm so sorry!"

He shook his head. "You didn't know. Again, I'll leave this for Anastasia to explain. Though, I do wonder what exactly she told you to get you here. Sidney is our Mum's advisor. He's like that stuffy old uncle you put up with. Sometimes he's okay, but often you just try to sneak the other direction when you see him coming."

Jamie let out a humorless laugh. "I know the type. As for how your siblings got me here? I've been wondering that for the last twenty-four hours or so. With the time difference, I'm not really sure how long it's been. She just said something about the ring, and asked if I'd come out for a vacation." She shrugged. "I really don't know why I came…what I'm doing. I have a life in Chicago, a good one…this is all just so fantastical…"

"What you are doing, m'lady, is getting a tour of the grounds. So, let's move on. Over this way is the archery field."

"Archery? Do you all shoot enough to have a permanent field?"

"All of us? No. Anastasia? Yes. She's very good with a bow and arrow. So…I guess, don't piss her off?"

CHAPTER 12

Anastasia followed her mum and Sidney. She watched as Adrian led Jamie away and wished she could be giving the tour instead of trudging into the house. Her day had been long, and this had all the tells of getting much longer.

She slipped into the palace, ignoring the grand entrance with the twin staircases and grand crystal chandelier. Sidney turned his head as he angled to the left, leading them up the stairs and to the family rooms. "Let's go to the formal living room. We can relax with some tea and cake."

Her mum dropped back and slid her arm around Anastasia's waist. "I missed you, Anastasia. I'm glad you're home." Anastasia took a deep breath, relaxing with her mum's words.

They followed Sidney until they reached their destination. Decorated in pale green and terracotta, there were two cream couches and three comfy chairs. Though she normally found the room's decor relaxing, today Anastasia felt out of sorts. She slipped away from her mum, and headed to one of the chairs. Sidney and her mum sat at opposite ends of a couch. A servant came over with a cup of peppermint and chamomile tea and offered her a plate of petit fours.

Anastasia sighed, put two small cakes on a plate and placed it on the table next to the chair. She took a sip of tea. "Okay Sidney, what's wrong?"

Before he could speak, her mum sat up straighter. "I'd like to start by telling you, before you even left, I knew who Jamie was. I remembered her from our trip all those years ago. How could I not? The two of you were inseparable. Then, while you were away, Adrian, who also thought he remembered your best friend from America, with her magical s'mores, went searching our records for something he remembered from his royal studies. That brother of yours has the memory of a steel trap. He brought that information to me and I presented it to Sidney."

Sidney looked uncomfortable as he reached over to the table next to him and grabbed a black folder. *Where did that come from? How long have they been planning this? Whose idea was it that Adrian take Jamie away? Wait…what is the situation?*

Sidney slowly opened the folder as he crossed his legs. "While you were off finding the ring…you did secure your royal signet, didn't you?"

"Yes, as crazy as it sounds, after fourteen years, Jamie still had the ring. She hadn't sold it or lost it or anything."

"Good, good. As your Queen mentioned, an issue was presented to me from the original decree of the land. Let me read to you what it states. 'Ixica will be ruled by the Royal Leader. He will yield the Royal signet and lead the people of the land to prosperity.' I would read more, but I feel you see the issue we face."

Anastasia rubbed her forehead. "Are you taking the words in that literally, like, I have to be a 'he', or marry a 'he'?"

Her mum scooted forward on the couch. "Don't get angry at Sidney darling, these documents have been the ruling doctrine of the land since Ixica won its freedom all those years ago."

"But Mum, when they were written, times were different. No one will care if I don't have a king by my side."

Sidney's face hardened. "You can *not* just decide to change the rules to suit yourself, Princess Anastasia. I am sorry, these laws have been our guiding principles, and people outside the three of us know of them. They are public knowledge. You can't just decide to ignore them."

Anger burned deep in her gut. She placed her tea down before she broke the delicate porcelain. She made a fist and hid it in her lap, shooting daggers at Sidney with her eyes. "But Mum is running the land right now, and last I checked, she is no 'he'."

He ran his finger down the page he had open, staring through the spectacles over his eyes. "Ah yes, here it is. 'In the case of a widowed Queen, she can rule the land without the presence of a King until such time as her eldest daughter marries or her eldest son is old enough to take over.' So you see, the wording wasn't a mistake. They truly meant for the land to be watched over by a king."

Anastasia narrowed her eyes at him. "So, what you're suggesting is I marry some unlucky bloke, get him offed, and then I can live my life the way I want?"

Sidney blanched, but her mum chuckled. "You could just have a mistress, Anastasia, like most royalty who are unhappy with their betrothed. I don't know why your first thought is killing off the poor soul. You've been watching too many horror movies. I knew they'd warp your mind."

She smiled at her mum and shook her head. "I wouldn't ask anyone I loved to be a mistress, or anyone I married to do it in name only. It all seems ugly."

Her mum leaned back, brows coming together. "How long have you been interested in girls?"

"I've always preferred women to men. Probably since before I gave Jamie her and my first kiss all those years ago. The better question is, how have you never noticed?"

Sidney closed the folder and placed it on the table. "This is all very interesting, but your affinity for women will not do. We have a country to think about, a King to find, and your mum would like to step down. You are being selfish, Anastasia. Find a husband, a King, and stop your selfish silliness."

Every word felt like a slap to her face, and anger roiled within her. She wanted to scream at him, but knew it wouldn't help. The pain of her nails cutting into her palms helped her focus on the words she needed to say as she stood and faced him.

She gave her mum a gentle smile, then turned to Sidney. "You are an idiot. I *will* marry for love and my 'affinity for women' is not something that gets turned on and off, you nitwit. If you and this country are so hell-bent on it having a King, fine, then talk to Malcolm. I quit!"

She spun on her heel and walked out with all the aplomb she could muster, though she wanted to run screaming, find a wall and start punching it. She'd trained to take over the throne from the age of eight. No one had ever told her about the necessity of a king at her side to fulfill her obligation to her country. The idea sickened her, as if she weren't good enough to rule without boy bits.

Malcolm and Adrian had done a bit of training too, but not as much as she had. Malcolm wouldn't be happy about becoming King, but he'd just have to suck it up.

I will not marry a man!

CHAPTER 13

"So, there's a private pool behind this hedge and line of trees?" Jamie tried to see the thick foliage, but could only see more leaves. "In the winter is the pool visible?"

Adrian, leaning against the house, tilted his head. "No, there's a wood fence as well as the natural one. We can go see the pool, but it's a bit cool for swimming. Maybe tomorrow. I was thinking of a bit of an indoor tour before we meet the others. We could slip in this side door; I have the code. You could see the residential hall on the main floor, then we could sneak into the kitchen for hot chocolate and biscuits."

She scrunched her nose. "You make biscuits? Or are they something from a box?"

His brow furrowed and he gave her a strange look. "You Americans are a strange lot. You know, a dessert?" He pulled out his phone and after a minute showed her a picture.

Eyes widening, she smiled. "Oh! Cookies. You're talking about cookies! I'd love some cookies with hot chocolate. That sounds delightful."

"Well, m'lady, let's head inside." He pushed off the wall and stepped forward to take her hand.

They entered the palace after he keyed in his private code. "Welcome to the royal mudroom. If you'll scrub your feet on the rug, I'll show you in."

The mudroom led to a windowed room facing the pool on the west side of the palace. The sunset smudged the sky over the trees behind the pool area in a stunning display. On the far edge of the pool was a waterfall and to the left was a covered daybed, at least queen sized, with tables for drinks on either side. Closer to the house was an inset hot tub, benches with pillows, chairs, tables, trees, flowers—a full outdoor living space. To the right there was a kitchen with a grill and what appeared to be a wet bar.

Her jaw slack, Jamie gaped at what had been described as simply a pool. "That's amazing. You could live out there."

Adrien cleared his throat. "This is the sun room; if you look up, you'll see it spans the full height of the house."

Jamie spun, tearing her focus from outside to inside. The sun room, with the black iron lined windows and open, airy space took her breath away. "I don't know how much more I can take, Adrian. This place is too much to believe… and you live here?"

"Come on, we're going upstairs. The first floor is the public floor. The second and third of the easter wing is for the family."

He led her through an opening to a grand hallway and immediately to a side door to the stairs. From there they went up a flight and through another door to another grand hallway. This one she had time to see. The carpet was a dark green with a white border and small white and pink flowers. The walls were lined with framed paintings of portraits. "Are the paintings the people from your family? The past Ixican rulers?"

Adrian smiled, lighting up his face. "Yes. Most of them go back generations, but eventually we'll get to my parents." He paused, gazing down the hall and back at an opening that overlooked where they'd come from. "If you look through here, you'll see the pool and the sun room again. The rest of this floor is for day-time shenanigans."

"Shenanigans?" She smirked.

"Oh yeah! Great word, no? Came across it during my time at University." He grabbed her hand. "Anyway, that's the best part! Okay; to the left we have a music room, a home theater, and a craft room. There are a few other things, but those are the interesting rooms. On the right is a family room, game room, and study."

"What do you consider 'not interesting'?"

He ducked his head. "Well, there's a library."

Jamie's jaw dropped and she bounced. "A library, like a private library? Is there fiction and nonfiction? How big is it?"

Adrian lifted his hands. "Okay, okay, I give up. I shouldn't have skipped over the book room. Would you like to see it? About a third of it is on this floor, and the rest is on the ground floor. I was hoping to get to the kitchen myself."

Jamie slumped and with a big sigh, relented. She had to admit she was tired and her mind already whirled with everything she'd seen on the tour. "It's fine; I'll check it out on another day when I have time…and not stuck with a luddite who doesn't appreciate the room. Let's go find these biscuits of yours."

Blue eyes twinkling, Adrian gave her a winning smile. "Perfect. This way m'lady."

She rolled her eyes. "What's with these 'm'lady' things? I'm just an American visiting. You're the one who's actually royalty."

He opened his mouth, then it snapped shut and he shook his head. After he took a few steps he looked over to her. "Again, this is a discussion you must have with my sister."

She sighed. "Every time. What is this big secret…no I

know, 'ask Star.' Let's just go to the kitchen. Let me take in the beauty of the palace."

They slowly walked down the hallway and she studied some of the images in the pictures. The ceiling was painted with murals of the sky and clouds. As they moved down the hall, some of the paintings were interspersed with paintings of trees with their branches reaching up into the sky.

Suddenly the hall opened up to a foyer. Jamie stood at the top of a large set of twin staircases that lead to her left and right, beginning by her and ending on the other side of the foyer a level down. They both circled a huge crystal chandelier. Across from where she stood, on the lower level, was a set of huge doors. *This must be the front doors where I started this crazy tour.*

Adrian stopped next to her. "Halfway there. The other half of this floor is for running the country, minus the throne room, which is on the first floor. On the left we have the formal living room, formal dining room, and the day room. All of those are for when we have guests. I'm not counting you as a guest, m'lady. Then we have the family dining room. On the right are a conference room and some smaller meeting rooms, all very boring."

Her mind spun as she tried to take it all in. "I can't believe this is your home." She realized she repeated herself.

"Come on, let's go."

As they crossed to the other side of the foyer, the hallway's carpet stopped with the end of the residential hallway and turned to inlay marble. The paintings on the wall transitioned to landscapes and abstract masterpieces. There were a few portraits, but they were few and far between.

At the end of the hall, Adrian pushed open a door and led her into a huge industrial kitchen with stainless steel counters, a large refrigerator, an eight-burner stove, four wall ovens, what looked like a deep freeze, and a small table that would easily seat six people. Currently, Star sat there, stuffing ice cream into her mouth.

CHAPTER 14

Anastasia stared at Jamie and Adrian as they walked around the kitchen, the spoon halfway to her mouth. She'd come here to be alone, and now she had to deal with Adrian.

He knew...that's why he immediately grabbed Jamie for the tour that I should've taken her on. Has he been laughing at me? Does he think I'm a fool?

Ice cream about to drip to the table, she stuffed the spoon into her mouth and glared at her brother. "I thought you were on a tour of the grounds?" She hated the snide tone of her voice, slumping further into her seat as she shoved the spoon into the tub of pistachio.

Jamie spun and gave her a big smile, then walked over. "Can I join you?"

Adrian jerked before turning. "I didn't see you in here, Anastasia."

She ignored Adrian and gazed into Jamie's dark green eyes, losing herself for a moment. "You can always join me, though I may be poor company."

Jamie took the seat next to her, sliding an arm around her waist. "What's wrong? You were in a much happier mood before my mind-bending glimpse into your world."

Unable to stop herself, Anastasia rested her head on Jamie's shoulder. "I just learned some pretty bad news and I'm not sure what I'm going to do, that's all."

"I'm sorry for what I found, sis." Adrian flopped down in the chair across from them. "I didn't want any of it to be true, and I really didn't want them to be the ones to tell you, but as soon as I showed Mum, she did her switch to Queen-mode and forbade me to contact you. I wanted to warn you, but couldn't. When you three got out, Sidney said that he needed to-" he dropped his voice to imitate their advisor. "Talk to the future Queen. Could I make myself useful for a spell and take the guest on a tour of the grounds." He shook his head. "That man can make me feel three inches tall like no one else."

Sitting up, Anastasia noticed Adrian brough some

bowls. "You think I'm sharing my ice cream?"

"I can hope. Maybe with Jamie, if not me."

She reached across the table and grabbed a spoon from his pile. "This should be enough. Why dirty the bowls?"

Jamie gave a single shoulder shrug. "I was promised cookies...um, biscuits. We could make ice cream sandwiches, if these cookies actually show up."

Adrian leapt up and walked away. "Oh, I really like her."

Jamie faced Anastasia. "So, what *is* this horrible news?"

Heart in her throat, Anastasia felt cold dread shiver through her body. She'd waited too long; she had to tell Jamie everything. "The ring you gave back to me, the one that signifies our engagement, the promise that one day I'll marry you?" Jamie nodded. "Well, according to some history Adrian dug up—and Sidney happily threw at me—I have to marry a man."

Jamie's eyes widened and all color had drained from her face. "So, this really *is* just a vacation after all. You won't be forced to pretend to like me, huh?" Her voice was neutral and she held her body still.

Anastasia placed the spoon back in the carton and shook her head, taking Jamie's hand. "No, that's not it at all. I think when I met you all those years ago, I gave you a piece of my heart. I know you don't know me, and I don't know you, but every time we touch it's like my heart stops for a second trying to match itself to yours. All I'm asking is that you give me the two weeks you agreed to, and stay to see if this is something you may want, too."

Jamie sat silently for a few minutes, mouth opening and closing. Then she grabbed her spoon and took a big bite of ice cream, closing her eyes as the cold treat filled her mouth. Jamie's eyes snapped open when Adrian sat down. Jamie grabbed the biscuits and made herself a sandwich. Once done eating it, she nodded, licked her lips, and sighed.

After a few minutes, Jamie rubbed her hands over her face then faced Anastasia. "This is a lot to take in. I…I really like you. I feel the connection too, but I have a life back in Chicago, a job, friends. You're going to be Queen, apparently with some man. Where would that leave me?"

Across from them, Adrian scooped ice cream onto a biscuit. "Be a Queen with her? Fight for this." He sounded sure of himself when he said these words.

Anastasia froze as it felt like someone dumped ice water on her head. She shook her head until she could get the words out of her mouth. "No."

Jamie's head snapped to her. "Wait, you don't want me to marry you. I mean, I'm not trying to push this, but… now you're confusing me."

Making fists until her nails bit into her palms, Anastasia gazed first at Jamie, then Adrian, then back to Jamie. "Adrian, you know there's a law in Ixica…that's what Sidney wanted to tell me. Ixica must be ruled over by a King." She turned to Jamie. "I do want to marry you...at least, that's what every feeling in my body is telling me, but the country can't be led by two Queens. We'd be royalty, but not the rulers, I stepped down from the succession. Malcolm will be the next king of Ixica."

CHAPTER 15

Jamie answered her door. A servant stood prim and proper wearing black trousers, a perfectly ironed white shirt with gold trim, a purple and gold striped tie, and an Ixican seal on the pocket. She brought Jamie appropriate attire for the day. A pair of tight pants that were similar to exercise pants with no center seam, purple on the inside and gold across the waist and down the outside of each leg. The servant also pushed a cart with a selection of black leather boots. She waited while Jamie slipped into the bathroom and put on the pants so she could try on the boots to find a pair that fit. It took her a few minutes to wiggle into the tight-fitting pants.

Once the bottom of the outfit was figured out, both pants and boots alike, the servant offered her a long sleeved t-shirt in the same purple as the leggings and a white, purple, and gold jacket she could move in easily.

She squinted at herself in the mirror, then at the servant. "Why all the purple and gold?"

With a wide smile, the servant said, "It's the royal colors, m'lady, plum and gold. If you'll follow me, I'll take you to the lady Princess Anastasia."

They walked down the hall to the doorway opening to the stairs. The bedrooms were all on the third floor, so Jamie traversed the main floor before she made it outside. Star waited for them by the hedge, head tilted up into the sun, a serene expression on her face.

When the door clicked shut, Star turned towards them with a smile and her eyes lit up. "Oh Jamie, you are the sight! Look at you in our colors! Thank you, Tracy." Star took Jamie's hand and they headed towards the stables. Two horses were saddled for them, a roan mare and a black stallion with white spots on the back legs and rump.

Star turned to her. "Do you know how to ride?"

Nerves bubbled up from her gut and Jamie's face warmed. She shrugged. "I rode when I was young and at camp. I think I can stay up in the saddle."

Star gave her a warm smile and slid her arm across her

shoulders. "Bring Jamie a helmet, and let's get going."

Her nerves shifted from nervous to mortified, burning in Jamie's gut. Her face heated further as she strapped on the black riding helmet. She even needed a servant to help her up onto the roan horse. But, quickly enough, she and Star were off towards the trees and trails. She'd expected an escort and was surprised when she checked over her shoulder and saw they were alone. "Will they let you out of their sight, *your highness*?" She waggled her brows teasingly at the last two words.

Star snorted. "We'll stay on palace property, so yes, we'll be free to roam, but if we go far and they find out, that's it for our galavanting about." She waved her phone to indicate how they'd track the two of them.

They spent the next few minutes clearing the field until they reached the shade of the trail in the trees. Jamie was glad they didn't signal the horses to do anything faster than a walk. She began to feel less nervous atop the beautiful creature.

Once the grounds were out of sight, Star faced her. "Tell me, what do you do in Chicago?"

The trees didn't look *that* different from back home, and the sounds of the birds were lovely. *Is there anything in my life back home worth discussing?* "Well, I work for a company as a project manager. I can help lead, organize, and determine the finance of…well, different projects. I'm actually pretty good at my job."

With a slight laugh, Star shook her head. "No, not that, I found all that on the internet. In *my* free time, what there is of it, I like to practice archery, I volunteer at the primary school working with the younger kids, and sometimes volunteer at the animal rescue center. I love to bake, but I'm not very good. Things like that. What makes you *you*, Ms. Jamie Woods?"

"Oh, that. Not the job. Well, I like to read. I go to my local library a lot. I'd buy more books, but my apartment isn't big enough. I like to ski and I started to learn how to snowboard last winter. In the summer, I like rollerblading and sitting by the pool, or the lake, doing nothing."

"I can get behind that last one. The pool is a lovely place to spend time. Did Adrian put that on his grand tour?"

Jamie shook her head, thinking about the palace and the place this family called home. "I can't believe all the things you have at your fingertips. Yes, I saw the pool. I hope we get to spend time there, and maybe the library. It all sounds like a spa vacation to this Chicagoan!"

"Yes, we can do it all. Since I've abdicated the throne, this will absolutely just be a nice vacation for you." Her voice was light, but there was a tightening in her shoulders.

Apprehension gripped Jamie and her muscles tensed. "I can't believe you did that. Are you sure that's what you want? You've spent your life preparing to take over the kingdom. Don't you want to fight for it?" Somewhere deep down, Jamie had begun giving in to her yearning for the soon-to-be queen. She'd decided to throw caution to the wind and let these two weeks play out, but she really didn't want to ruin Star's chance at the future she'd spent her life preparing to live.

Star held her body stiff as she said, "Sidney made it sound like a done deal."

"But what about—" Her horse jerked from under her and Jamie went flying, landing awkwardly on her hip. Her head banged hard against a rock, and the stupid helmet she hadn't wanted to wear saved her from worse injury. Slumping down, she gazed through the leaves, so reminiscent of the ceiling on the second floor of the palace, and stared at the perfect cerulean sky above dotted with perfect white clouds.

"Oh my! Jamie! Are you okay?"

Jamie sighed. "I'm fine. The silly hat you made me wear seems to have performed its job admirably. But, can we wait a few minutes before getting back up? Maybe walk around a bit?"

She heard Star moving above her. "Okay, the horses are secure, can you get up?"

Jamie pushed herself up to sitting, then took off the helmet. She handed it to Star before she rose on her feet. The transition to standing was a bit shaky, but Jamie felt fine despite the fall. Star grabbed her hand and led her through the trees and down a hill. Before long they were by a small lake. Jamie sat in a grassy area, soft and clear of rocks, and gazed at the pure blue water. "This is lovely."

"It's one of my favorite places to come think. I haven't been here in awhile, things have been too busy, but you chose the exact right spot to be thrown to the ground."

Jamie snorted. "Glad I could be so accommodating… though some of the credit could go to the horse…I guess."

The two sat side by side for a few minutes, enjoying the stillness.

This is vacation…and more like a dream than reality.

Jamie twisted to face Star and slowly leaned in, giving Star a chance to back away. Heart pounding, Jamie let her lips touch Star's. At first, Star froze, and then her mouth melted against Jamie's with a faint groan.

She felt Star's hand curl into her hair as her tongue traced her lips. Tendrils of heat flowed to her core as Jamie opened up, reveling in the feel and taste. Star's tongue began to investigate her mouth and Jamie groaned, leaning in closer.

Star's other hand moved to Jamie's side, her thumb slowly rubbing the side of her breast. Breath coming in shallow gulps, Jamie's hands landed on Star's hips.

Pulling back, Star smiled at Jamie. "Have you ever done this with another woman?"

Body tingling, Jamie could barely focus with Star's thumb moving on her breast. "Um…No, not really."

"Are you sure you want to do this? Now?"

Staring into the sparkling blue depths, Jamie nodded. "Yes. I've wanted this for a while now. Since I first saw you in Chicago."

Star slowly unzipped Jamie's jacket, pushing it off her shoulders. She pulled out the bottom of Jamie's shirt, tugging it off and dropping it to the side. Her bra quickly followed. She pushed Jamie down on the grass and hovered over her, leaning down to kiss her deeply again. With a moan, Star broke off to slip out of her own clothing.

Shivers of anticipation shot through Jamie. Reaching up, she pulled Star down, tasting her again, rejoicing in the feel of the other woman's warmth against her own. Muscles low in her abdomen tightened with need and she let her hands explore the soft contours of the woman above her.

Star's hot kisses moved from her mouth down to her ear where she nibbled down the side of her lobe. Jamie's body vibrated with a tight desire like she'd never felt before. Arching up, she tried to get more contact with Star.

A line of heat trailed down her neck and over her collar-bone as Star moved to Jamie's breasts. The moist heat of her mouth sucked in one nipple while her hand played with the other—a sweet torture. Jamie's hands dug into the grass and dirt as jolts of sensation shot from Star's mouth and hand throughout her body.

Just as Jamie thought her head would spin away, Star's

tongue and mouth sizzled up her body until she hovered over Jamie. Her warm breath tickled Jamie's ear. "I really want you naked."

"These pants are so tight; do they come off? I thought I'd been dressed for the duration of my visit."

They both laughed as they wrestled with the riding pants and underclothes and then used the shirts and jackets as a blanket. Straddling Jamie, Star twined her fingers through her hair and gazed down into her eyes. "Let me know if you want me to stop."

Every nerve in Jamie's body sang; she couldn't imagine what would cause her to want any of this to end. Nodding, she lost herself in the feel and motions of the woman above her.

As Jamie writhed on the ground and her breath caught as Star's mouth descended, kissing along her torso and abdomen until it finally found the juncture of her legs, where Star's tongue lapped at her clit. Jamie closed her eyes, gasping in shock. Her body jerked as heat built in her belly and pulses of electricity tingled down to her fingers and toes.

Then she felt a finger pushing inside her. Small gasping sounds filled the air as a second and third finger joined the first, and Jamie realized it was her. Star's teeth replaced her tongue, and then Star sucked. Jamie's body lifted off the ground as a whirlwind of feelings rushed through her. Sex had always been good, *but oh my god!*

The tsunami of pleasure exploded and Jamie screamed,

the world fracturing around her. Her eyes closed as a rainbow of colors passed across her vision and wave after wave of sensation pulsed through her.

Star slid back up to lie next to Jamie, collapsing onto her back. "I've wanted to do that for days."

Jamie curled into Star. "What about you?" She asked breathlessly. "Can I reciprocate?"

CHAPTER 16

It had been two nights since Jamie's arrival in Ixica, but Jamie agreed to sleep in Anastasia's room. As Anastasia woke and stretched, the sun played across Jamie's curls. Anastasia gently brushed them from her face and bent to give the sleeping beauty a kiss. Waking up next to her felt so good...right, somehow.

After untangling themselves from the bed and dressing, they headed down to breakfast. When they got to the family dining room, Anastasia was surprised to find her mum—as well as both her brothers and Adrian's friend Finley—were all up and there as well. It was early for such a crowd. Usually everyone sauntered in at their own pace. Finley and Jamie had met at the pool after their horse ride the day before, the two guests enjoying the relaxation of the hot tub.

Plates of eggs, bacon, and pancakes were placed in front of everyone, as well as mugs of coffee and glasses of orange juice. The cooks were trying to make Jamie more at home with the American style breakfast.

"How was your trip? Have you enjoyed our grounds? Your horseback trip?" Sipping her coffee, her mum gave Jamie a friendly smile.

Jamie swallowed her bite of pancake, closing her eyes in apparent bliss. "Everything has been wonderful, thank you Ma'am. Your palace...your home...it's all beautiful. I can't imagine living here. The horses...well, I have a bit of learning there."

"Oh? Your ride wasn't pleasurable?" A single brow rose.

Jamie blanched, and Anastasia had to slap her hands over her mouth to stop herself from spitting out her coffee. She felt both her brothers' eyes on her as she tried to swallow her laughter.

She looked up in time to see Malcolm lean back in his seat. "So, sister, a side trip on your ride yesterday?"

Jamie made a strangled sound, before taking another bite of her pancakes.

With a shake of her head, Anastasia laughed and turned to Jamie. "What else do you want to do during your visit, while my *brother* is learning what it'll take to become the next king of Ixica."

Malcolm's head hit the table and his muffled voice could just be heard. "God, I hate that you've stepped down. We're going to talk about this later!" He threatened.

Finley sipped his coffee. "I think this is the best laugh I've had in a while, personally. Better than any joke Adrian or I have played on you."

Malcolm glared at him, before returning to his food. Finley seemed to sink into himself a bit.

After taking a sip of coffee, Jamie glanced at each of them, before stopping on their mum. "I'd love to see the throne room and the library; both rooms were left off my initial tour. I'd also like to spend time by the pool, it looks so lovely out there."

Mum's face lit at this. "Delightful. After breakfast you and I, and maybe Anastasia, will head to the library, it's my favorite area of the palace. Then we'll see the throne room. From there, you two young love birds can do whatever it is you want." Her eyes narrowed and her head shifted to Anastasia. "You Princess, need to fight for your rights, if your heart is still in the throne room. You've spent your life training to take over the country. You, with your brothers, should take this to the people and hear their opinions of this antiquated law."

Body numb with her mum's words, Anastasia just

stared back agape. *Fight back? Was that possible? Sidney made it sound so impossible!*

With a sigh, Adrian shook his head. "That's what I've been trying to tell her, but she wouldn't listen to me."

Malcolm, eyes a bit crazy with hope, voiced her questions. "Weren't the papers Sidney showed us the final word?"

Mum's face tightened as she stared at them each in turn. "Yes and no. The people have the final word. Let them know what we're facing. I believe we have a bit of wiggle room, not much, but let's hear what they have to say."

Adrian stared off into space, no doubt thinking about all the laws of their country. He'd been training to take over as financial advisor and had studied many of the old covenants. "Okay, Malcolm, Finley, and I will set up a royal brief for the town square in three days. That should be time enough to get the word out."

Could I really be Queen and have Jamie? Her heart skipped a beat at the thought of having it all.

After that, the discussion switched to talking about favorite books. Once breakfast finished, Jamie, Anastasia, and her mum headed down to the throne room in the east wing on the first floor.

A set of stairs outside the kitchen brought them down to the main hallway that led back to the front entrance. After they'd passed the first business room, a second hall led north towards the back of the palace and to the throne room and ballroom.

Two large doors, fifteen feet high in the center, sloped downwards at the top for the width of the wide doors, eight feet wide each. The doors were embossed with intricate geometric patterns and had guards standing outside them at all times.

As the party approached, the guards opened the doors for them in unison. The long and vast room glowed with the morning sun streaming in from skylights above. Murals decorated the walls on either side of the room, and a dyed concrete floor presented the Ixican seal.

Jamie slowly circled the room, mouth slightly open as she gaped at the splendor all around her. As she finished her circuit, she returned to Anastasia and gazed up to her. "You can't give this all up, it's too much. Isn't this singing in your blood? Your soul?"

Licking her lips, Anastasia surveyed the room with fresh eyes. She'd been in the room so many times. The raised platform at the far end with the main throne and two smaller seats, one for the queen and a second one brought in for her to learn. The images along the walls depicting Ixican history. The grandeur of everything around them. *Can I give this up?*

She placed her hands on Jamie's shoulders. "The better question becomes, can I represent a people who won't allow me to be myself? I'm not marrying a man, Jamie; it isn't me, and that is what they—the covenant—are demanding. I will see what the people say. If they want a king, then, yes, I will give it all up. I won't live a lie nor ask someone else to. Not when I have brothers who could lead and lead well."

A small "Oh!" escaped her before Jamie tensed, then smiled shyly.

Shortly after that, they went to the library. Again, Jamie was lost in the room that spanned two floors. Though many of the tomes were old and focused on Ixica and its history, there were other books as well. A section of paranormal, urban fantasy, and high fantasy books—both with and without romance—that the librarian filled because of Anastasia's interests. Historical fiction and high fantasy for Adrian. Horror and thrillers for Malcolm. There was even a section on action and technology for Finley. He'd practically lived in the palace during the summers over the last ten or so years. They all read each other's books, tending to just like to read a good book. There were many books they hadn't yet read; the librarian loved to support both traditionally and independently-published authors, filling the shelves with anything she thought would be read.

Jamie walked through the shelves, touching the books with a far off look in her eyes. Anastasia feared losing Jamie here for the duration of her visit.

While Jamie searched the book stacks and corners of the library, Anastasia's mum pulled her down in one of the reading nooks. "I really like her, Anastasia. I hope you figure this out, but do understand the long distance thing will be difficult. And as a Royal Princess, even if you'll never achieve the throne, you must stay in the country."

Her head fell back, hitting the seat cushion hard. "I know mum, I know."

CHAPTER 17

A hand rubbed up her leg over her...oh! Up her belly to her chest. It spent a bit of time gently investigating before she found herself being kissed.

Jamie opened her eyes to see Star and a warmth filled her. The sky behind her darkened to a deep blue with the oncoming of twilight. Wrapping her arms around the beauty above her, she deepened the kiss.

Star laughed, pulling back. "I just wanted to wake you up, my lovely Jamie. We fell asleep by the pool and we have a date to go dancing with Malcolm in town tonight. Unless you want to go in our swimsuits—which would make quite the spectacle—we need to go change."

They headed up to Star's room and stripped from their suits, and moved into the bathroom for a shower. Star's ensuite bathroom was about the size of Jamie's full apartment in Chicago, with a huge shower that could fit half a volleyball team, a jetted tub big enough for both of them, two sinks, and an airy, open feel that allowed for free movement. High above them, windows let in the lowering sun.

After the showers they each put on club clothes. Jamie slipped on a pair of tight black jeans and a black tank top. Dark eye makeup and red lips finished up her look.

Once done she sought out Star and found her in wine leather pants and a black leather halter top. Her black hair was in a high ponytail, small braids leading up to the ponytail encircled her head. She'd painted her face with dark makeup.

Jamie stood agape, heart pounding in her chest, unsure if she could breathe. Finally gulping in some air she said, "You look great."

Smiling with a twinkle in her eyes, she said, "You too. Let's go find Malcolm."

Malcolm waited for them by the front door wearing black leather pants and a tight black mesh shirt. His gaze traveled over them, eyes narrow, before he nodded with a smile. "That will do." Then he led the way out the door.

Outside, a dark green car that looked expensive sat

waiting for them. Malcolm opened the back door for them, and Jamie slid in first. The first thing she noticed was the car was set up just like an American car. She thought back to the limo, and realized she'd hadn't seen the driver through a divider. Once Malcolm got in to drive she asked, cheeks heated. "You didn't mention people drove on the same side here as they do in Chicago."

He shot a look at her over his shoulder. "You didn't ask, and it was too amusing watching you squirm."

She huffed. "What type of car is this? It's beautiful."

Malcolm hummed in appreciation. "This is my baby, Sage Nightstar, she's an Aston Martin Rapide. I don't let anyone else drive her."

They headed down the drive and towards town. Star grasped her hand. Lights behind them had Jamie checking over her shoulder. "Are we being followed? Do the people follow you around? You'd be pretty recognizable in this car."

Star, who had been watching Jamie, quickly shot a look over her shoulder as Malcolm chuckled from the front seat. "That's our security detail. Like I said, off the property we're never alone."

Jamie's brows furrowed. "What about in Chicago?"

"They were there, just more discrete." Star explained. "They like to give us the feeling of freedom, even when it isn't a reality. No one knew we were traveling so we were relatively safe."

When they arrived at the club, Malcolm slid into a spot with a reserved sign for royalty. Getting out of the car, flashes snapped in her face. Jamie recoiled and froze by the car, until Star and Malcolm took each of her hands and led her into the club. Shouts from the crowd flowed over them as they moved through the flashing lights.

"Malcolm, Anastasia, who is she?"

"Who's your guest?"

"Anastasia, when's the coronation? When will you be crowned?"

"What's the town gathering about?!"

The club was dark and loud with lights that flashed different colors. They squeezed their way through the crowd to get to the bar. Malcolm leaned over the bar to speak to the bartender. A few minutes later he returned with three drinks.

They found a table, and Jamie sipped her drink. It went down smoothly and she realized how dangerous Malcolm's order was. He was as dangerous as Emma in ordering drinks. She could drink these all night not realizing how much alcohol she consumed. After about half her drink, the siblings dragged her out to the dance floor.

As they danced, people came out to join them. They came to dance near Anastasia and Malcolm. Sometimes they tried to say something, yelling over the music, but Jamie couldn't hear a word uttered. The large smiles and waving arms showed the lack of communication didn't bother anyone. It seemed the people of Ixica just enjoyed socializing with the royals. Song after song, the three of them danced, gyrating and waving their arms, moving and swaying.

Adrian sashayed up with Finley. His height stood out in the club and his dark auburn hair was styled for a night out. They both wore tight pants and dark button down shirts. Different locals joined them for different songs and moved away, mostly women, mostly focusing on Malcolm, Adrian, and Finley.

Every few songs they moved back to the table to get refreshments. Though Jamie kept drinking, her glass never seemed to empty. As her head swam and her inhibitions lowered, she learned more about Adrian's friend. Finley was from England but spent many summers in Ixica causing havoc and mayhem with Adrian.

Finley and Adrian tried to drag Jamie out to dance again. She shook her head. "I'm beat. Go, have fun, I'll watch."

Malcolm leaned over the table to be heard over the loud music. "You two enjoy yourselves, I'll take the old ladies home."

Finley looked disappointed. "You're not going to leave me alone with this chap are you?" His British accent was thick.

Adrian shook his head and held out his keys to Star. "I know how you are about your car, Malcolm. Why don't you let the ladies head home and you stay with us? You can drive us home when we're actually tired."

Eyeing the dance floor with delight, Malcolm leapt at the chance. Star took the keys, and she and Jamie headed for the door. Once outside, the deafening sound of silence hurt Jamie's ears almost as much as the pounding music. There were a few paparazzi, but security held them back. Star led her to a blue Lamborghini.

Shaking her head, Jamie glared at the car. "Does everyone in your family own a ridiculous car?"

Sliding behind the wheel, Star began adjusting the seat and the mirrors. "The boys do. I'll give them this much, these cars are fun to drive. Are you really too tired to do anything but sleep?"

Jamie smiled at Star, trying to be seductive, but not really knowing if she could pull it off. "I am tired, too tired to dance…on a dance floor. But I may be convinced to do some *other* kinds of dancing."

Hitting the gas pedal, Star took off for home.

CHAPTER 18

"**O**kay sexy lady, your turn."

"I've never done this before; you'll have to show me."

"You're doing great. Just breathe out…and release."

Anastasia felt Jamie's body tremble as her hand opened and the arrow flew. She lowered the bow as they watched the arrow fly over the target into the apple orchard. A moment later there was a juicy *thunk* sound from the direction her shaft had flown.

Jamie slumped. "You make this look so easy. Your target is dead in the water, every shot practically a bullseye. My attempt is lost in the woods."

Anastasia knew Jamie was frustrated. They'd been out for over an hour, but Jamie didn't see how much she'd improved. She had a natural stance, and from the start, she could get an arrow cocked and flying in the right direction. Anastasia feared if she gave too much encouragement, then Jamie would think it was false flattery.

With a laugh, Anastasia took her free hand. "Let's go discover where your shot landed."

"My shot? Why, it's probably in some clump of grass…long gone."

They tramped through the woods until they found the arrow stuck in an apple hanging from a tree. "See? A perfect shot! Too bad it wasn't on William Tell's son's head, you could've been some sort of literary hero!"

Jamie finally laughed, and Anastasia felt her relax as her shoulders dropped. "Okay, fine. My attempt wasn't completely horrible. But, can we stop this for now? Don't we need to get ready for your big media event?"

Anastasia checked her phone. They had enough time, but she'd let Jamie use that as an excuse. They headed back to the palace to get ready. Because they were a bit early, they could shower…together, which Anastasia had to admit was time much better spent than practicing with bow and arrow

Casimir had sent some dresses to the room for them to wear. Hers was gold with a plum hat, jacket, belt, and shoes. Jamie had a similarly cut dress in plum, with the same plum belt. There were gold panels in the skirt that became visible when she moved. Her outfit didn't have a jacket or hat; it was less formal.

Once dressed, they were escorted into a limo with Adrian, wearing a black tux and the standard gold and plum tie. "Are you ready? Do you have your talking points for today?"

She gave him a hard stare. "Are you really asking that?" She knew he was joking with her, but it wasn't helping. She'd spoken to her people before, but nerves still played havoc with her system.

He grinned. "I know you're ready; this is just really important. You're the best choice to run this country. Can you imagine Malcolm as king?" Adrian visibly shuddered and an answering chill ran down Anastasia's back.

She loved her brother, and in all honesty, he could be a great King if he had his heart in it, but it wasn't anything he wanted. She and Adrian always loved learning about ruling Ixica, but Malcolm has other loves.

When they made it through the crowds, they found Malcolm overseeing the staff and ensuring everything was in place for the event. Squinting, Anastasia took note of who set up the event with him. "Is that Finley helping out?"

Adrian snorted. "Malcolm complained that he'd be more hindrance than help, but Finley insisted. Finley's a computer whiz; he'll make sure all the tech stuff is working the way we want it."

Her heart pounded and her fingers tingled as the minutes counted down. She took deep breaths as she watched Adrian walk on stage to start things off. Jamie wrapped her arms around her from behind. "You'll be amazing. This is your time, Star, just remember that."

Adrian's voice reverberated over the sound system. "Good morning, people of Ixica. I am happy to see you all gathered on such short notice. Our family has learned some new information—or maybe, I should say relearned some old information—and we wanted to bring it to you for discussion. For the details, I present my sister, Princess Anastasia, and one of her friends, the Lady Jamie Woods."

Jamie lost all color in her face when she was mentioned. Adrian calling her name hadn't been in the original plans, but Anastasia loved the idea of having the two of them standing there together. It was the image she wanted to present.

Twining their fingers together, Anastasia slowly walked up the steps and across the stage to the podium and the microphone. Though Jamie hesitated at first, she followed, supporting Anastasia, which let her breathe a bit easier.

She gazed over the mass of people there to listen to the situation she found herself in. "As you all know, I am slated to take over for my mum—to be the next queen of Ixica." She paused for the cheers and applause. "What some of you may or may not know," she took to breath to let her nerves calm, "my choice of who will join me isn't a king… but rather, another queen."

She stood a bit taller at those words while the crowd seemed to pause, taking a collective gasp. Then, slowly, scattered groups began to clap. More and more people joined them, making sounds of support: applauding, calling out, and cheering. Warmth grew in Anastasia's soul as she realized the people supported her even if the decree of their nation didn't.

Once the crowd quieted, she continued. "I was reminded of the decree of Ixica which states: 'Ixica will be ruled by the Royal Leader. *He* will yield the Royal signet and lead the people of the land to prosperity.' I have been told this means I have to marry a man, that I—as a woman—am not good enough to rule without a king. I ask you, the people of Ixica, to join with me to help modernize our country. These laws were written so long ago, and we are a progressive people who understand that one doesn't need to be a man to rule this country."

The cheers erupted from the crowd, chantings of "Queens can rule" and "Give Anastasia her Queendom."

Jamie's hand felt cold in hers, but when Anastasia looked over, she had a big smile on her face. She mouthed, "I'm so proud of you."

She was about to continue with her speech, when a

disruption came from the back of the crowd. A man with a megaphone interrupted the chanting. "It's not that easy, Princess Anastasia. I am Richard Felie from the Archives, and I have proof of why what you ask is impossible!"

CHAPTER 19

The words punched Jamie's gut as the crowd mumbled in confusion. Who was this "head of the archives" to say it was impossible? It wasn't that she wanted to be Queen, run a country, or be any type of royalty, really. This whole trip felt like a cross between a dream and a delusion. In the end, she wanted Star to have her fairytale ending.

Like ice cold water, this man's words sent a chill down her spine and brought her back to reality. She tried to stand tall and proud—be everything Star needed—but her eyes misted with the realization that everything was crumbling, and in front of a crowd…all the Ixican people…Star's people. They believed in Star, but if what this man said was true. How many obstacles were there?

Star squeezed her hand and squared her shoulders. "Mr. Felie, if you'll come around to the back, we'll discuss your proof. As for the rest of you, thank you for coming out today. We'll keep you informed as matters develop. It has never been—and will never be—our policy to keep anything from you. I appreciate you all coming out today to support the Ixican Royal Family." She lowered her head in a slight bow before turning and leading Jamie from the stage.

Once out of the public view, her shoulders slumped. Star gazed at Jamie and her look said she didn't want to admit defeat, but it felt like there were obstacles at every turn. Turning to her brothers, she said, "Malcolm, Adrian... get me out of here. Make sure someone gets Mr. Felie to the palace...What the hell just happened?" The last was mumbled under her breath.

The five of them, including Finley, piled into a limo, and Malcolm handed out glasses of mimosa. Star drank hers quickly and then had a second. "That was a complete mess. Who is Richard Felie? The archives? Why didn't we go there before holding this public farce? What a mess!"

Jamie watched, her head spinning, as Star's trembling subsided. It felt like Jamie's world was on a topple over every other day routine, and she was ready for it to stop. How long ago had it been, that all she worried about was a job interview? And then Star showed up...

Adrian reached over and squeezed Star's knee. "It wasn't that bad, sis. We'll go home and see what he has to say. He obviously knew what we were going to announce. I wish he'd come to the palace prior to our event instead of making a scene in public. If I find out he tried and was held back, heads are going to roll." He turned to Malcolm. "Text Sydney, make sure he and mum know what's happening."

The limo pulled into the circular drive and stopped in front of the doors. They got out and Star took control, directing the servants. "When Richard Felie gets here, show him to the main conference room. Have coffee, tea, and snacks brought there at once, as well as the Queen and her advisor."

As they headed up the stairs and to the conference room, Star turned to Finley. "Can you do your computer magic, see if you can find records of this man?" He smiled and ran up the stairs at a jog.

It didn't take long for the servants to bring a cart carrying refreshments from the kitchen. They'd all found seats along the long table in the main conference room and waited for the meeting to begin. Jamie, sitting to Anastasia's right, signaled the footman for coffee and a sandwich. Her mum and Sidney came in and found seats that faced the door a few minutes later.

The last to arrive was Richard Felie, the archivist, carrying a briefcase. He stared at his feet as he came in and took the first seat, ignoring the others in the room. The man was squat with a long face, thick brown hair, and dark intelligent eyes covered by glasses. He jerked when a servant approached him asking what he'd like to drink. "Tea, black, two sugars, milk if you have it. Do you have any food? I'm starving."

Once he had a plate to stave off his hunger and a fancy teacup full of tea, he began pulling papers from his satchel, continuing to ignore everyone else at the table. Jamie tilted her head, impressed at his indifference at sitting in a room full of royals. Jamie still felt a bit of nerves, and she wasn't Ixican.

Star cleared her throat. "Mr. Felie, welcome. I am curious and looking forward to hearing what you have to present to us."

He jerked and finally gazed at the others at the table and the color drained from his face. "Oh my, Queen Rebecca, your Majesty, beg your pardon, I hadn't realized you'd be here." He shot up from his chair and performed what Jamie assumed was a bow. "I'm sorry for my disrespect."

Rebecca—Jamie still had a bit of difficulty thinking of the queen by her first name, but that was the request, and that's what she'd do—smiled at the man. "You don't feel my children are deserving of your respect, Mr. Felie?" Jamie bit her cheek to stop herself from laughing. The Queen's brow shot up. "Please sit so we can get this all figured out."

Mouth opening and closing, he searched the faces of

everyone at the table before sliding back into his seat. "Yes, your Majesty, I mean, no, your Majesty, I mean…I believe they do deserve respect, especially since one of them will soon be taking over for you, your Majesty, my Queen."

Jamie tried not to react to his babbling, but it was difficult. Checking out the others, they all had blank expressions, staring at the man. *Oh no! Get yourself together Jamie! This is not the time to start laughing.*

Sidney cocked his head. "You mentioned proof. Please, explain yourself. Why did you wait until the assembly this morning to say anything?"

The man's jaw tightened and his face reddened, and Jamie knew it hadn't been his first attempt to talk to Star. "I am the head historian down at the Society of Archives." He pulled out a document and began to hand it to Sidney, but thought better of it and instead handed it to Star. "This is a copy of the declaration of formation of Ixica. Our country will be dissolved if we aren't led by a king. I tried to come to talk with your mum…er, the Queen. Even her reign couldn't have lasted more than a year without the danger of dissolution…not with you and your brothers of age to lead."

Adrian leaned forward. "Tell us exactly what your message is, Mr. Felie."

His hands shook as he took a sip of tea and he faced Star. "It isn't anything against you, Princess Anastasia. It has to do with Ixica's right to the land we own and our ability to stay a country. We are our own country, but the lands were given to us by another nation under specific conditions. If we mess up any of them, then we lose our lands and our rights and Ixica will be a country no more."

CHAPTER 20

Anastasia woke up early with a small smile seeing Jamie sleeping next to her. A small smile played across her face and a warmth filled her. She wasn't sure how she and Malcolm convinced Jamie to follow them back to Ixica, why this wondrous person had agreed to join her in her life, much less her bed—or how she'd been so lucky in finding her soulmate in a woman from the middle of America—but somehow, everything had come together.

Despite all the wondrous good, she still had a lot to think about, worry about, and decide on. She quietly slid from the bed, and headed down to the music room. She really didn't feel like playing music, but there she could think and move, and not inadvertently wake up Jamie. She sat at the piano, and just stared at the keys and thought.

She'd lived her whole life knowing she'd take over the kingdom from her parents...the *king*dom. God, she never knew how pertinent that word really was. Did anyone?

What do I really want in life? Do I want to fulfill my life's mission, what I've spent over fifteen years training to become? Can I really give it all up? Sidney wasn't wrong when he said I could marry for state and have love on the side. The marriage could make our country stronger...politicians have been doing that since the dawn of time. Why do I think my marriage would be any different? Am I worth more than my country? Do I really think so much of myself to put me before Ixica?

She leaned back, resting her head on the wall. *Would Jamie be willing to be nothing more than a mistress? If not, could I find someone else who makes me feel the way Jamie does?*

The thought of losing Jamie bit deeply into Anastasia's gut and a tear burned down her face. "No." she said to the quiet room.

"Talking to yourself, sister mine?" The door opened and Malcolm slipped in. Still in his pajamas, his tousled bed head hair looked good. It wasn't fair he always seemed put together. *Sporting a just woke up look, Malcolm...* He draped himself over the couch.

Anastasia quickly wiped the tear away, trying to hide any emotions from her perceptive brother. "What do you want, Malcolm? It's early; I thought I could have a few minutes of peace."

He sat up, leaning forward with his elbows on his knees. "We need to talk."

One of her brows lifted. "And what are we doing now?"

"No, seriously, we need to talk, Star." His shoulders sagged. "I can't do it. I started my lessons with Sidney, and I can't do it. I know we each did some basic training before, but I never thought it would lead to anything serious. Please sis, don't make me fulfill this crap. I can't. I have a job, a life…the situation I'm in is one I rather enjoy, and it doesn't include running this country."

Heat began burning through her system. "You want me to live a lie because you'd rather make outfits than run this country? You, who can live whatever life you want regardless of what you're doing? You'd stuff me in a closet like the clothes you love, just so you can continue to make them!?" She was nearly screaming at the end.

He leaned forward. "Is it just Jamie? I remember you dating some blokes in your past."

"Those were set-ups by Mum and Pa and you know it. I've never chosen to date a guy in my life. 'Is it just Jamie?' yes and no." She stopped. Moving. Breathing. Imagining life without the dynamic woman was too much. "No, she's more than a 'just' to me." She gazed off into space for a few seconds, unable to imagine life without her American soulmate by her side. Softly, she admitted to her brother, "I love her. I don't want to know what my life would be like without her. It's not worth it, none of it. The throne, ruling, any of it. Losing her is like tearing out a piece of my heart."

His head drooped. "Have you told her?"

"I don't want to scare her off. Loving me comes with a lot of baggage. If she knew how deeply I felt, she'd be on the next plane out of here, away from the looney bin that is our lives."

Malcolm pushed himself to his feet and held a hand out to her. "Well, we'd better go find Mum and give her the news."

They walked to the family dining room and sat for breakfast, a tradition their mum had kept over the years. As they ate, they explained their final decisions to their mum.

With a small smile, she said, "Have you proposed to the girl, my dear?"

Coffee halfway to her mouth, Anastasia gaped at her mum. "Proposed? To Jamie?"

Her mum's eyes twinkled. "Why, yes, dear, that would be the next step. I know you're new to all of this, but the only way the girl knows you want her to stay in your life is if you tell her. She's not a mind reader…is she?"

Shaking her head, trying to get her mind working again, Anastasia mumbled, "No." Then searched the room, as if Jamie were hiding. "Has she come in for breakfast?"

"No dear, I haven't seen her this morning. Why don't you go look for her?" With a small smile, Anastasia knew when she'd been dismissed.

She stood and the servants came to clear her plates. She decided to start by checking in her room. A lightness filled her with the decision finally made. When she finished eating she made her way up to her rooms, but they were empty. About to head out, she stopped and took a closer look, they weren't just empty of Jamie, they were empty of all Jamie's belongings.

After searching the bathroom, the closet, and the receiving room...she found everything had been cleared out. Jamie was gone.

CHAPTER 21

Jamie woke up to a still room—quiet, and empty. When her hand dropped to Star's side of the bed it felt warm, so she must not have missed the Princess by much.

To sleep or to follow. She stretched and decided she'd have plenty of time to sleep once she returned to Chicago. *I should savor as much of this fantasy life as I can. It's almost at an end, anyway.*

Checking her email, she saw the second round of interviews were in four days, and she'd made the cut. She also had a text from Emma.

You'll make it back in time, won't you?

This job had been her world for two and a half years. *Of course!*

She leaned back against the wall and bit the inside of her cheek. *I'm not lying to Emma...to myself, am I? I am returning to Chicago...right?*

She slipped from the bed and dressed in jeans and a t-shirt. *Well, I may not know my way around this palatial place* – she chuckled at her own internal joke – *but she must have gone down to the second floor. There's pretty much only bedrooms up here.* Turning towards the sunroom, she headed for the stairs and the second floor.

As soon as she exited the closed stairwell, she heard Malcolm and Star arguing.

Star sounded worked up, yelling at her brother. "You'd stuff me in a closet like the clothes you love, just so you can continue to make them?"

Malcolm's response was cool, sounding calculated. "Is it just Jamie? I remember you dating some blokes in your past."

The blood pounded in Jamie's ears. *Star's dated both men and women? Am I just some fanciful fling before she gets on with her life? She's trained her whole life to become the Queen of Ixica. Why would she give it up for me, some idiot American? God above, I've been a fool!*

Turning, she fled back to the stairs, running up them two at a time until she got to the bedroom she'd shared with Star for the last week. She stuffed her clothes and toiletries into her bag, picked up the room phone, and asked for a servant to come up to help her.

A few minutes later, Tracy, one of the few maids she knew by name, came in. "M'Lady, how may I aid you?"

"Something has come up. Is there any way I can return to Chicago? Today?"

Tracy's brows came together, as proper as everything else about this place. *Why did I think I could fit in here?* "Of course. We can have a car bring you to the airport and the royal plane can return you to your home immediately. Should I call for–"

Jamie threw up her hands. "No, please, don't interrupt them. They're all busy...very busy today. I can do this on my own. I think my bags are all packed; can we just leave? Please?"

Her insides were slowly being turned to stone, one step at a time. She tried to stop the tears as they gathered in her eyes, but she couldn't. A second servant came to carry her bags, and they handed her a plum handkerchief with the royal seal. She clutched it in her hand as she followed the two servants out. At the car, she stuffed it in a pocket, a token of her fairy-tale adventure.

She felt a bit giddy at making it to the car without seeing Star, her brothers, their mum, or Sidney. This was for the best. If she left, they could build their life back the way it was supposed to be. She wasn't important enough to ruin Star's life...and possibly the entire future of Ixica.

The trip back to Chicago was uneventful. Despite what Tracy had promised, Jamie bought a ticket and flew home on a regular commercial airline home. The plane ride was lonely without Malcolm or Star to keep her company. At the airport in Chicago, she hailed a cab back to her apartment. She texted Emma along the way, telling her she'd be back at work the next day.

Back at her desk, she finialized the organization of her desk and work. *This is where I belong…where I'm meant to be.* An email arrived, asking if she'd be willing to move her interview up to that afternoon. With a half smile, she shrugged and sent an email to accept.

Emma burst into her office. "Oh my god, I can't believe I'm actually looking at you!"

Her friend's exuberance cut through a bit of her melancholy, and she smiled. "Hi Emma. It's nice to be back. You won't believe the email I just got."

Emma flopped into the chair across from her desk. "Spill."

"They want me to interview today."

Emma's eyes grew to saucer-size. "What? But you just

got back. Are you ready? Can you do it on such short notice? You'd think they'd give you twenty-four hours for good behavior…you have been on good behavior haven't you?"

Jamie snorted. "Mostly…I guess. I mean, I didn't cause a big enough international incident to make the news here, did I? Wait, did I?" A sudden chill of concern washed through her. The press conference they held was just the kind of news gossip rags in the US loved. Emma didn't usually go for that type of thing, but if she'd been watching for news from Ixica…

Though Emma held a solemn expression for all of four seconds—her friend had no poker face—and she started to laugh, holding her gut. "You should see your face, friendo. What did you do that you're so worried about?"

Sighing, Jamie shook her head. "Not here, not now. We can go out for dinner tonight and talk if you want, but I'm not going to get into gossip…*about me*, at work."

Emma narrowed her eyes and looked at Jamie as if this were the worst news she'd heard in a long time. With a huff, she finally agreed. "Fine, I guess—but we're going out to dinner tonight and you *will* tell me about this trip of yours…oh, and the interview."

Jamie began to feel better. She sat up taller and smiled. She'd missed her friend, even though she hadn't realized it due to the distractions of her trip. "Deal!"

After Emma left, Jamie struggled to focus on work. Her

mind kept returning to Ixica and a certain royal Princess. She began to feel guilty for leaving without talking to Star, though she didn't want to ruin Star's life, the one she'd been building for so many years.

When she got call from the executives to come up for her interview, she closed her eyes, took a calming breath, and tried to release anything that wasn't going to help her to become a project manager.

Two hours later, she headed home to get ready for dinner with Emma.

They had sushi. She wasn't surprised when she saw Emma invited Tucker; she'd missed both her best friends.

Emma pointed at her with chopsticks. "You are an idiot, you know that, right?"

Jamie took a bite of her black dragon roll and thought about her friend's sage evaluation. "An idiot?"

Tucker sighed. "Star isn't going to suddenly marry some man and take back her kingdom. I wasn't even there and I understand that. Did you even listen to your story? Were you even paying attention?"

"I don't want to ruin her life. She's spent years training to be Queen of Ixica. I don't even know how much she cares for me." She stared back and forth between her two best friends trying to get them to understand.

Emma's eyes narrowed. "Idiot. You are a first-class American idiot. It's probably because you love her and you're afraid of rejection. But, you need to call her, beg her forgiveness, and stop being dumb."

Jamie nearly choked on her next bite. "What are you talking about? I barely know her."

Emma's head dropped to her hand as if she could barely take any more. "Honey, I've known you for years. Please don't pretend I don't know you better than you know you." She straightened and the chopsticks were back, pointing accusingly at her. "These are the emotions you didn't have with Charlie. This tsunami of doubt and hope and...dare I say it again...love. You love her. I'll give you twenty-four hours, then I'm stealing your phone."

Dread washed through Jamie. "You wouldn't."

"Wouldn't I?" A smile spread over Emma's face even the Joker would envy.

CHAPTER 22

Anastasia's feet dangled in the water as she debated what to do next. Jamie had left her. She had no idea why.

Water splashed her and she looked up to see Malcolm in the pool. "Stop being so mauldin, sis. Either get over the American or do something about it."

Water hit Malcolm and he spun to retaliate against Adrian. "You would attack your King?" His voice rose ominously by the end.

Adrian smiled wickedly. "You're not King yet, brother, and once you are, happily! Someone has to keep you humble." He turned to Anastasia. "Change your mind, sister. We can not live with him like this, it's too much for his feeble mind. The power will corrupt him and he'll wither into something no one will want to witness!"

"That's it!" Malcolm yelled, diving for Adrian, and they both went under. Anastasia shook her head at their antics. They'd been wrestling in the water their whole lives. Before they could pull her in, she stood and moved to the hot tub, letting the warm water melt away some of the tension she held as she thought about Jamie. *Why didn't you even leave a note? Or text? Or call?*

Thomas, one of their servants, brought her a glass of wine as she sunk lower into the warm water. Before he walked off, she asked, "Did you see Jamie leave?"

He bowed slightly. "No, your highness. But I believe Tracy was with her. Would you like me to fetch her?"

Anastasia debated, but finally nodded. "Yes, please go find her for me."

The water jets massaged her legs and back and she tried to escape her worries for a few minutes. Eventually, a soft voice interrupted her. "How may I be of service, Your Highness?"

With a sigh of contentment, she opened one eye and considered the servant. "Did you speak with Jamie before she left?"

Tracy bowed. "Yes, Your Highness. She said she had to get back for work—it was an emergency. She didn't want to interrupt you or your brothers. She felt you were all too busy. Maybe she saw you two in the music room? I did see her coming up the stairs a bit earlier."

Hope and dread fought within her. Was that a lie? The truth? A bit of both? When they'd picked her up in Chicago, there had been that interview, so there may have been something big that suddenly came up. *But why didn't she tell me?* A nasty part of her psyche asked. *Because she was scared? Felt trapped?* She had no idea and guessing wasn't helping.

"Thank you, Tracy. You may return to your duties."

Tracy spun on her heel and headed away just as Malcolm and Adrian slid into the hot tub.

Anastasia glared at them. "No rough housing, I'm trying to think and you two are distracting."

Adrian tilted his head. "What big thoughts are you having, sis?"

She bit her lip and explained what she'd learned.

Malcolm nodded. "What if she'd heard us in the music room...or part of what we'd been yelling at each other. Enough to think leaving would make our lives easier. She goes, you go back to being queen and I no longer need to be king. She may also have something big happening at her work, but the timing fits."

Adrian glanced back and forth. "And what exactly were you fighting about?"

Malcolm explained.

Adrian shook his head. "When are you going to grow

up? You're going to be king soon, so hopefully before then."

Malcolm slumped so only his head was above the water. "Easy for you, you're not being dragged from your desired life to the throne, a lifetime commitment."

Adrian's face hardened. "Enough. Anastasia, you need to go after Jamie."

Scrunching up her face, she rolled her eyes. "Why?"

He snorted. "Because you love her and will be impossible to live with until you get this taken care of."

"I wha...huh...you can't...wha..." She couldn't get out a coherent sentence.

Malcolm sat up, chuckling. "Why brother, she's finally speechless. I like this side of her." He grabbed her hand under the water. "Repeat after me. You love Jamie."

She stopped trying to talk and just gaped at him, jaw hanging open.

He lifted his free hand to tap her chin and close her mouth. "This will never do. Let's go find mum. Maybe she can talk some sense into you, Star." He turned to Adrian. "She seems to have lost it."

Filing out of the overhot water, they wrapped towels around themselves and found their clothes in the sun room. After quickly dressing, they headed to the throne room where they approached the Queen.

She gazed down at them, mouth tightening at the sight of her children and not another of her petitioners. She turned to the side. "Sidney, are there others who require my time?"

Standing at the side of the room in a suit, chin high, a look of disappointment on his face, Sidney checked over his notes. "No, Queen Rebecca. Your last petitioner just left."

Anastasia stepped in front of her brothers, a tightness in her body. "You don't think we would've made sure you had time before entering this room, Your Majesty?" At the end she performed a curtsy. Out of the corner of her eyes, she saw her brothers bowing.

Her mum sat a bit taller in her chair and tipped her chin down. "What are you three doing in here?"

Adrian moved up to stand beside Anastasia and bowed again, deeper. "We seek your council, Your Majesty. The Lady Jamie Woods has returned to Chicago before Princess Anastasia could discuss any future partnerships. As the future advisor to the next King and Queen, it is my opinion that she rectify this situation. However, Prince Malcolm can no longer travel as chaperone; he has loftier responsibilities. I request a leave from my duties to escort my sister in this endeavor."

Behind them, Anastasia heard Malcolm snort, but she kept her focus on the Queen's face. As Adrian spoke, she kept her face blank. Finally, she narrowed her eyes. "You want to fly to Chicago with Princess Anastasia so she can propose to Lady Jamie because the girl ran off when none of you were paying attention?"

Adrian nodded slowly. "Yes."

She sighed. "Do you think she'll say yes? Do we know why she slipped off in the first place?"

Nerves playing havoc in her body, Anastasia placed her hands on her legs to stop from fidgeting. "We were informed something came up with her work. I am hoping that if I let her know the seriousness of my offer, it will convince her to decide moving here is more important than her job."

An imperial brow rose. "She seems like the kind of woman who finds having a career important."

Her mum's words punched her in the gut. *Of course Jamie would want to feel useful living here. What was I thinking? Come here and what? Just be pretty? I've been such an idiot!* She had to work to keep her mouth from hanging open. She couldn't get air as she wracked her brain trying to come up with an answer to an impossible question. What would Jamie do?

Adrian placed his warm hand on her shoulder. She shot him a nervous look before returning her focus to her mum. All his attention was on the Queen. "I believe we can find her a job here at the palace. I've been running the schedule and budget for the royal family, but with the rise of social media and the internet, the job has grown and we haven't grown with it. I believe a project manager would be the perfect addition. From what I've seen, part of her degree was in finance; she could probably do my job. I believe she'd be an excellent leader within my team."

At his words, Anastasia gaped at him, not believing what she heard. Adrian had done his homework, predicting what their mum would ask. He winked at her before blanking his face to await the Queen's response.

Gulping in air, she spun back towards their mum as well.

Her mum's face finally softened. "Alright, my children. Go off and follow through with your machinations."

Anastasia's heart pounded. "What about the wedding?"

With a small smirk, the Queen tilted her head. "Jamie has to say 'yes' first."

CHAPTER 23

Jamie sat in her office, feeling a bit numb, but deciding that meant she was in the zone. She riffled through the projects that needed her attention and set up priority lists. The interview two days ago had gone well, and she wanted to make sure everything in her current position was completed in case a miracle happened and she got the promotion.

It had taken time to clear away tasks from her time away; go through emails, and remedy any errors made by the person who'd tried to keep up with her responsibilities, but she was starting to feel back in the groove. Despite conquering a mountain of work, tension built in her shoulders and back. She debated taking a walk, maybe getting a coffee before the pain migrated up into her head and she developed a headache.

"Have you taken a break since returning from fantasyland?" Her head snapped up at Tucker's voice.

He stood tall in her doorway, his light blond curls somewhat contained. As always, he wore a fashion-perfect suit—today it was light gray with a jewel blue button-down. He could've walked out of a magazine.

"What are you doing, slumming down here? I never see you outside of la-la land?"

Emma slammed into him, curling her arms around him from the back. "He lowers himself to our level. I didn't know he knew our lower floors existed."

He wrapped an arm around Emma's shoulders. "Well, my lovelies, I had a break, and though we could head out for coffee, to that truck you so love."

Jamie leaned back in her chair, tilting her head to consider him. "Isn't the coffee up in la-la land excellent? Why would you want to go out to the truck?"

His face broke out in a smile. "Let's just go and get coffee, my friends. This floor is giving me hives." He made a mock horrified expression and lowered his voice. "How do you two survive?"

She and Emma laughed, gathered their purses, and headed to the elevator.

As the elevator sped down, Tucker crossed his arms across his chest. "Have you contacted your Princess?"

Jamie raised an eyebrow and mimicked his position. "Have you found yourself a queen?"

He held his position for a few seconds before he burst out laughing. "Oh, I've missed you. No, like your Charlie, my Prince Charming keeps slipping through my fingers. Unlike you, I know I want a man in my life."

Emma leaned against the back wall. "Don't we all?"

Before anyone could answer, the doors slid open, and the three headed out. At the coffee cart, the owner gave Jamie a big smile. "My favorite customer, back again. I thought you'd given me up for something much worse."

Hand slapping her chest, Jamie gave him a tragic look. "Never. You make the best caffeinated salvation around… and you are correct, anything else would be unthinkable."

He smiled. "Large black with a splash of milk?"

She sighed. "That sounds like heaven."

Jamie grabbed her cup and headed to a small table as her friends ordered their complicated dessert drinks that probably contained some coffee in them—somewhere. Once they joined her, Tucker leaned forward. "The bugaboo upstairs is Jamie is a shoe-in for the promotion. The emails are going out later today. You'll be up top with me. We just have to figure out how to get Emma elevated, and our takeover will be complete."

Jamie's heart skipped a beat. "So soon? The interviews just happened. Don't they need a week or three to mull it over?"

His eyebrows danced. "From what I heard, they only had three people in for the second interview. They really wanted you from the start, my friend, but had two backups in case you flubbed it up beyond repair."

She took a pull from her coffee, enjoying the flavor. "I'm glad you didn't tell me that before that second interview, talk about pressure!"

He winked, but before he could answer, a ding from Jamie's purse had them all pause. She lowered her chin as she gazed at the bag trying to remember how to breathe.

"You're killing me, babe." Emma shook her. "Check your phone. It could be from the big decision-makers upstairs letting us know our little Jamie has risen in the ranks."

She took a shaky breath and slid her hand in her purse until she reached her phone. Swiping it on, she found the email, but couldn't get her mind working to read it. "You read it, I can't." She waved the phone over the table at large.

Emma took it before Tucker could. Her eyes flew over the email, best poker face in place, giving away nothing. With a smirk she looked up and then froze, focusing on something behind Jamie's back.

Annoyed, Jamie glared at her. "Ha ha, Emma, tell me what you saw."

She shrugged. "Royalty?"

CHAPTER 24

Anastasia and Jamie drove up to where she knew Jamie worked. As luck would have it, she saw Jamie sitting with two other people drinking coffee – a shorter redhead with crazy curls cascading down her back, and a gentleman with light brown curls that framed his face. *With Jamie's curls, they could form a curly haired gang. Maybe that's what attracted them together in the first place. Maybe they have club jackets.* Anastasia had to bite her cheek to stop from laughing. She was a bit loopy from lack of sleep. She and Adrian had been up since they'd decided to leave, packing, planning, and traveling.

They all stared at each other for a minute, before Jamie shot to her feet. "What are you doing here?" Her face turned red and she made fists with her hands. "I mean, it's lovely to see you of course, but you have a country to run. You should be doing queenly things, not standing in front of me in Chicago." She dropped her chin to her chest, her shoulders slumping. She mumbled low, probably thinking Anastasia couldn't hear her. "That's why I left...so you could have your life back."

Anastasia wanted to shake sense into Jamie, and scream at her, but mostly, she wanted to hold her. She reached out to tip the crazy woman's chin up, forcing Jamie to meet her gaze. "You, Jamie Woods, I hope, will *be* my life. I love you, and would very much like to build a new future with you, if you're interested."

The pretty man sitting on the other side of the table mumbled, "I knew it!" He lifted his fist and the redhead bumped hers to his with a smirk.

Jamie began to tremble. "But what about all your training? What about becoming queen?" She bit her lip, her eyes large and hopeful.

Anastasia shifted her hand to cup Jamie's cheek. "I don't want the position if it means I can't be the person I want to be, be *with* the person I want to be with. I have two brothers, they are both good people...mostly." She snickered. "Malcolm will make a good king, despite his belly-aching. We've all trained for it, and though I've done most of it, he knows what is expected of him."

"But what about–"

From behind her, her friend hissed. "Stop thinking and kiss your Princess, Jamie. You know you want this, we both told you she wanted it, too. Stop being a ninny."

The sharp-dressed man snorted. "Emma's correct, get out of your mind, and listen to your heart, girl."

With a small nod to her friends, Jamie turned back to Anastasia, eyes shining with determination. Anastasia watched as Jamie stepped forward into her personal space, placing her hands on Anastasia's hips. "I love you too, Star. I think you've had my heart for years." She tilted up her head and Anastasia caught her mouth in a kiss.

Anastasia wrapped her arms around Jamie, pulling her in tight, deepening the kiss for a moment. She became lost in that second, that millennia, that lifetime.

Pulling away, the talking of the others slowly penetrated her mind and she smiled. Adrian introduced himself to Jamie's friends, smiling at the man, and kissing the woman's hand.

She focused on Jamie, and something clicked. When she held Jamie, she knew that this was right. She knew this was what she wanted. Taking a half step back, she held Jamie's hands and gave them a small squeeze. She took a deep breath and said slowly, but clearly, not wanting to mess this up, sunk to a knee. "Jamie Woods, will you marry me?"

CHAPTER 25

Jamie stopped breathing. Behind her, both Emma and Tucker squealed. Her entire world telescoped down to the gorgeous woman standing before her and holding her hands. *Did Star just ask me that? Did she mean it? Is it possible?*

She licked her lips, then opened her mouth, but nothing came out. *I want to say yes, but what would happen to me if I move to Ixica? Would I take up embroidery? Underwater basket weaving? Gardening?* A shiver threatened at the thought of any of those activities. Would she atrophy as Star's pretty royal wife?

Desperate, she tried to speak again, but again, no

sound came from her.

She heard Tucker's sound of disapproval coming from behind her. "She's stuck in her head. What do you think it is, this time?"

Emma hummed. "Who knows. Familial expectation. Job promotion. Relocation. Knowing her, it could be anything. Hey Jamie, do you love her?"

Jamie nodded slowly.

Tucker chuckled. "Do you *want* to marry your princess?"

She hadn't stopped nodding and she didn't see any reason to end after that question. Her eyes never left Star's as her friends grilled her.

Adrian's voice came from near Star, a bit softer. "Are you worried about what you'll do in Ixica?"

She wondered how he'd read her mind and froze for a second before nodding again. Finally finding her voice, she replied. "I want to marry you, but I don't want to be useless. I have friends here, a job here, maybe even a promotion."

"You do have a promotion, silly." Emma said, forever being helpful. "You're brilliant, how could you question it?" She waved Jamie's phone to emphasize how she knew about the promotion. "And we'll still be part of your life no matter where you live."

Jamie smiled, suddenly finding humor in her situation. Why would she need to work if she married into the royal family? Did any of it really matter?

Anastasia's hands moved up to her face, and she gave Jamie a chaste kiss. "If you want to work, then you'll work. Adrian's already figured out a job for you in the palace...and before you think it's a pity job, it isn't. He knows what you do here in Chicago, and plans on taking full advantage of your skills."

She glanced at Adrian questioningly and he smiled back. "The palace hasn't evolved with the technological advances of the twentieth century, much less the twenty-first. Trust me, we have plenty that could keep you busy. Hell, we could probably use two or three of you."

A lightness filled her and she felt like she could float away on a cloud of happiness. Her cheeks began to hurt with her smiles. She felt her body tremble as she realized her life was about to change. "Yes, Anastasia Tuffin, I will happily marry you...though I doubt I'll start calling you by your full name, it doesn't quite fit. You'll always be my Star."

Cheers went up all around them as Anastasia engulfed her in a hug. "I don't even know what to do next. Do I go back to work? Go home and pack? Drive home to Wisconsin to tell my parents? God, my parents!"

Tucker and Emma pulled her away from Star to give her a big group hug. Then Tucker booped her nose. "You should probably turn down the promotion and let someone else have a wonderful day. And telling your parents isn't a bad idea. Oh, and while you're at it—maybe introduce us to your new friends and fiance?"

With a start, Jamie quickly introduced everyone. They agreed to drive up to Wisconsin and talk with her parents. Since Malcolm hadn't come along with his obsession to drive, they had arrived in a limo. Emma and Tucker agreed to pack the basics for her, and insisted on returning to Ixica with her.

Narrowing her eyes, Emma pointed at her. "You can *not* expect to get married without us. Princess Anastasia will have her whole court, you will have us…and probably your parents. No arguments, Jamie." There was no mistaking the sarcasm at the last bit.

Adrian, staring at Emma intently, nodded. "That sounds logical to me. There is no reason your friends can't travel with us. There is plenty of room in the jet and at the palace. It will help you adjust to have them there… assuming they can take some time off work."

Emma smiled at the Prince. "I haven't taken any time off since I've started, so I'm good." She gazed up at Tucker. "You?"

One shoulder raised in a half shrug. "I should be good. And I wouldn't miss this for the world. Jamie finally getting married? Outstanding!"

It took about three hours to drive from Chicago up to her home in the suburbs of Madison, Wisconsin. The closer they got, the more nervous she felt. She hadn't been keeping her parents apprised of all the crazy that had been happening in her life.

On the drive up, she gave her mom a call to warn them she was arriving with some friends.

"Is there anything wrong, dear?"

"No mom." She said quickly, her mind too scattered to hold on to anything concrete. "I just…we need to talk. We'll be there in a couple of hours."

"Well, we'll have dinner made, is brats with potato salad and corn on the cob okay?"

"Sounds perfect."

When they pulled in front of the house, she led Star and Adrian up to the front door. She pulled the screen door open when her dad's voice floated around from the back. "We're in the back, Jamie. After you show your friends the house, come on back. Unless it's Emma and Tucker, then just come up the driveway."

She turned to look at Star and Adrian with a shrug. Star smiled warmly. "I'd love to see where you grew up— your house, your room, anything to know more about you. But if you'd prefer, we can just head to the back."

With a shrug, Jamie continued taking them into the house. It had two floors and she started them on the second, showing the two her old bedroom with her posters of alternative bands and unicorns. A bookshelf and small desk. The siblings immediately took stock of which books they'd read, and hadn't.

They then went down and got the tour of the main

floor before adventuring out back to the patio.

"Mom, Dad, this is Star, um, Anastasia, and Adrian. I don't know if you remember them, but we met them years ago when their family came…"

Her mom leapt up. "Oh goodness, you're the kids from Europe, aren't you!"

Star tilted her head in acknowledgment and Adrian laughed. He said, "We sure are. We came back looking for Jamie; we never could forget her and her delightful s'mores."

Both Jamie's parents chuckled at that.

Jamie tightened her fists and took a deep breath. "Mom, Dad… there's more." They both looked at her, and she froze, unsure what to say.

Star came up next to her and wrapped an arm around her shoulders. Adrian stood on her other side, providing a unified front. She knew then that these two would always stand with her; she wasn't alone. She'd always had Emma and Tucker, but now she had more than just friends—she had family.

With a steadying breath she continued with a small smile. "Star asked me to marry her, and I accepted."

Her mom squealed and a huge smile spread across her father's face. Over dinner, they explained the story of how the siblings found her, and who they were.

Her dad grunted. "You were who all that hullabaloo in the news was about. If I'd known *that* was who the Lady Jamie was everyone was talking about, I'd've paid more attention!"

Jamie didn't know if she should've laughed or cried, remembering how much her dad paid attention to the international news. At the end of dinner, her parents told her they'd fly out in a couple of weeks, closer to the wedding.

"We have some prior commitment here, dear, but we wouldn't miss this for the world." Her mom gave her a huge hug, then gave way for a bear hug from her dad.

When Jamie, Star, and Adrian returned to Chicago, they met up with her friends to board the plane to Ixica. Jamie hoped that the people of Ixica were ready for Emma and Tucker. They may not be staying long, but her friends always seemed to leave their mark.

CHAPTER 26

A nastasia stood in the center of her room. It felt empty without Jamie in it, and she smiled thinking about how she ended up bunking with Emma.

They were all in the sun room discussing the wedding. Anastasia and Jamie shared a love seat, arms linked. Emma and Tucker shared a couch with Adrian. Malcolm and Casimir each sat in chairs, and their mum had the other love-seat to herself.

Malcolm curled his legs up under himself. "So, the wedding is ready for next week, how long are the two of you planning on shacking up together?"

Casimir's eyes nearly popped out. "What? Oh no! That will not do. Ms. Woods, you will move out immediately until after the wedding. This is the royal palace, the royal wedding," he turned to Anastasia. "You are the Princess. Fix this, now."

Her mum smiled slightly. "Is it really that big of a deal?"

The wedding planner sat a bit taller. "You asked me to arrange a royal wedding, your Majesty, and that is what I'll do, but if you want it done correctly, you'll have to listen to my rules."

"Very well. It shall be done." The Queen's signal towards the servants had them scurrying towards the rooms in question. "Please have Lady Wood's belongings moved to a guest room."

Emma, who looked ready to burst out laughing, shook in her seat. She scooted forward. "Can she share my room? I'm sure she'll want to spend time with me before I'm shipped back to America."

No one argued the point and Anastasia's mum gave the servant a single nod.

The day of the wedding came faster than Anastasia thought possible. She hadn't seen Jamie for the last two days as the final preparations were completed. Any questions or concerns had gone through Emma and Adrian who'd taken over as Jamie and Anastasia's representatives.

A knock came to her door and Tracy entered. "Your Highness, I've brought you a light breakfast, then you're to shower and dress. Do you have any questions about your schedule?"

Despite the day being *her* wedding day, nothing about it was her own. Sitting by the window, Anastasia quickly ate eggs, toast, and fruit salad. She savored the coffee before slipping off to shower.

A hair stylist and makeup artist came to curl her hair and do her look. Afterwards, she stepped into her gown, a form fitting sleeveless white dress with a small train. She wore elbow length gloves and a star tiara. Casimir showed up to make sure everything was perfect.

The wedding would take place in the ballroom, and anyone who wanted to attend was invited. Both she and Jamie would walk down the aisle, but Jamie would walk down first, so she was stuck waiting.

Since her father had died, Malcolm, the next king of Ixica, would walk her down the aisle. Her brothers would each stand with her, and Emma and Tucker would stand with Jamie. They decided to have a small wedding party.

Two young girls and a boy from the class she volunteered in joined as the flower girls and the ring-bearer. The girls wore plum dresses and the boy a black tux with a plum shirt. Casimir and his assistance had spent days getting all the clothes and tapestries just right. Malcolm had wanted to help, but as future King, he'd been dismissed by Casimir, much to his chagrin.

"Heya sis," Malcolm walked in without knocking, as was his habit, wearing a black tux. He looked the spitting image of their pa and she could see the king he'd soon be. He took her in, his look analytical. "You look...well, amazing. Are you ready? Last chance to change your mind."

Her nerves had been gathering in her gut, but with his words she rolled her eyes and groaned. She gave a small chuckle as she said, "Enough, this is what I want."

He slid a hand around her shoulders, careful to not mess up her hair or outfit. "I know, Anastasia, I'm just teasing you. It's time. Let's head down. I'm guessing you're biting at the bit to see Jamie after two whole days being kept from her."

A small growl came from Anastasia. "This tradition is bonkers, if you ask me. One day you'll find your own Prince Charming, and you'll be put through all of this."

He smiled. "You think I'll let Casimir anywhere near my wedding?"

She tilted her head as they exited the room and raised her brow. "You think you could stop him?"

They continued to joke as they made their way down the stairs. The first floor was decorated with flowers and candles. They immediately stood taller, aware they could run into spectators at any turn.

When they got to the ballroom, which felt like hours later, the room was packed with as many people who could fit in the large room. More sat outside, viewing the proceedings through the open windows. There were a few cameras as well, televising the wedding. As soon as Anastasia and Malcolm stepped through the doorway, the music began and her heart pounded faster.

Despite the music of the four-person orchestra and the murmurs of the people, all she saw was Jamie. Her hair was pinned atop her head with curls cascading around her face. Small flowers were weaved in randomly, and she, too, wore a matching star tiara. Jamie's outfit was similar to hers, with a single shoulder strap, versus Anastasia's dress which was strapless. Jamie's dress had a higher waistline. Standing together, they would match.

She's stunning.

"Are we standing here all day, or are you going to walk down the aisle?" Malcolm whispered into her ear.

CHAPTER 27

Jamie's room smelled of the roses she'd walked through on her first day in this fantasy land. Earlier, Adrian delivered a bouquet from Star.

Emma observed as the stylist pinned Jamie's hair in place so that her curly waves cascaded down her back. For a finishing touch, Emma selected a yellow rose and twined it in her hair. Her hands were numb with nerves as she made her way back to the triple mirror that the servants had set up the day before at Casimir's directions. The mad-man had come in earlier to assure the gown adorned her curves perfectly.

Jamie stared at herself in the mirror. "Am I really

marrying a princess today?"

Emma came up behind her, wrapping an arm around her waist. "I know, right! This is crazy. And Tucker and I are here to witness it."

"I just can't believe you'll be living in this palace with that pool!" Tucker said from the other side of the room.

A knock came from the door and Tucker leapt to answer it. Her parents came in. They stood gazing at her. Her father spoke first. "Sweetheart, this is all so amazing. We're so happy for you…and you look beautiful."

Her mom rushed over to give her a careful hug. "I've brought a bracelet my mom, your grandma, gave me that I want you to have. Something old. The tiara is new."

Emma pulled off her gold necklace. It was a thin chain with a small blue sapphire in the shape of a heart hanging from the end of it. "You can borrow my necklace. It will count as borrowed and blue."

Her mom smiled. "Perfect."

Her dad came up and linked his arm with hers. "Are you ready, sweetheart? I think it's time for your big entrance."

They headed down to the main level. There were a few people hoping to get seats in the main ballroom rather than sitting outside. They didn't give her more than a fleeting glance, not knowing who she was. Once they got to the ballroom, the music began and the murmuring quieted.

Jamie and her dad followed the flower girls, students

from the class Star volunteered in. Behind them came Tucker with her mom and Emma with Adrian.

When they reached the end, they faced the Queen standing in a gold dress and plum robe with fake fur lining. She held a staff and wore a crown. Since arriving in Ixica, this was the first time Jamie had seen the Queen in her full regalia. She felt intimidated. She wasn't sure she could call this woman by her first name ever again.

Her dad kissed her cheek and sat next to her mom in the front row. Emma and Tucker stood behind her and Adrian stood smiling at her, leaving room for Star. He gave her a wink before turning away.

Taking a calming breath, she faced the people of Ixica. Blood pounded so loudly in her ears she couldn't hear anything. She hoped she wouldn't pass out before the ceremony started.

The Queen's voice cut through her nerves in a soft comforting voice. "Just breathe, girl. There'll be no fainting on my watch."

She tried to bite back a laugh as the music started up and everyone faced the back to stare at Anastasia and Malcolm.

They oozed royalty. He was king. She…God above, she was gorgeous. *And she wanted me?* Again Jamie marveled at her good fortune all those years ago, running into Star at the park near her house, the two of them daring each other to eat crazy foods, and finding a soul mate who happened to live so very far away.

Malcolm leaned down to whisper in Star's ear as Star and Jamie gazed at each other across the room, and then they started walking towards her.

When they reached her, Malcolm turned to the room in general, searching the faces of everyone. These were his people. "Who here agrees to let Jamie marry my sister, the Princess Anastasia Tuffin?"

Her dad stood, just like in their practice sessions. "I do, as her father, along with her mother. We agree to this marriage and offer our blessing."

The two nodded in a small bow before her dad sat and Malcolm took his place in line with Adrian. Star stood facing Jamie, eyes alight and dancing.

The Queen began the marriage speech, allowing each of them to recite vows they'd prepared in advance.

Star's thumbs traced the back of Jamie's hands in hers. "Jamie, when we met, all those years ago, my heart, my soul, knew you were my future. We spent years apart, but in the end, I was pulled back to you. I will spend the rest of my days learning the joys of who you are and what you bring to our fair country. I honor your strength of insight, as well as your heart and devotion to friends and those you love. I look forward to the years we have together."

As her Princess spoke, Jamie's insides knotted together. She had no idea how she would follow the lovely words that poured over her, like a warm shower of love.

Trembling slightly, she swallowed as she heard the Queen tell her it was time for her to speak. "I think I've been lost, and you found me. Each day of my life I was performing actions I was good at, capable of doing, doing well, but a part of me was numb, living a life of what I should be doing, not what my heart and being wanted to be doing. You entered my life like a dream and I feel like I'm still dreaming." A few people in the crowd chuckled at her admission. "I love you, not only for everything you are, but everything you see in me and have done for me. You are more than a brilliant leader of this country, you are a warm loving person who cares for others, when not aiming an arrow at them." Another round of laughter, a bit louder this time. Jamie swallowed, wanting to say all she felt. "I will spend the rest of forever in awe that a star as bright as you shines on me. I hope only to give you the same light back, lifting you as high as you lift me."

After the applause, they exchanged rings, kissed, and the room erupted.

Everyone reclaimed their seats and the Queen continued, "I present to you—the newest addition to the royal family—Princess Jamie Tuffin."

Please review to help other readers know to enjoy The Royal Entanglement Series!

**Continue to read about the crowning
of the next Ixican Royalty:**

Book 1: Malcolm and Finley's Story: Royal By Design:
https://mybook.to/RoyalByDesign
Book 2: Tucker and Casimir's Story: Royal Coronation:
https://mybook.to/RoyalCoronation

Find more information on my website:
https://hannahwillow217.wordpress.com

Find me on:
Facebook
TikTok
Instagram

Twitter

ACKNOWLEDGEMENTS

I want to thank the people who encourage me to write. Wes Imrisek, Elizabeth Daly, and Angela Grimes take my stories and make them more. They take my raw work, and help me to refine it into something better than I could do alone. The rest of my writers' group, the Confused Chaos, are there every day, getting me to laugh, write, and form better stories. I'll always be trying to keep up with C.C. Davies as she writes up a storm. Marleen Dekker and Kelsey Ortiz are the best beta readers ever. Fe Foster, Eva, Alice, Brian, Grant, and Jacinta are always there to help to refine my thoughts and ideas, making me a better storyteller. My son is always there to help me brainstorm new and crazy ideas as are the rest of my family when I suddenly ask off the wall questions.

I want to thank all my family, friends, and any of you who are fans of my writing. I love creating stories, and plan on doing this for as long as you want to read about my crazy characters and their lives.